The Matchmaker,
the Milliner
and the
Man from Maastricht

The Matchmaker, the Milliner and the Man from Maastricht

ALI SIMPSON

Troubador Publishing Ltd
Unit E2 Airfield Business Park,
Harrison Road, Market Harborough,
Leicestershire LE16 7UL
Tel: 0116 279 2299
Email: books@troubador.co.uk
Web: www.troubador.co.uk/matador

ISBN 978 1 80514 076 4

British Library Cataloguing in Publication Data.
A catalogue record for this book is available from the British Library.

Printed and bound in Great Britain by 4edge Limited
Typeset in 11pt Minion Pro by Troubador Publishing Ltd, Leicester, UK

Matador is an imprint of Troubador Publishing Ltd

For my husband David, who always believed I could.

Part One

IN ENGLAND

September

Hey Izzy

How are things? All okay here, just, but was feeling a bit blue so thought I'd say hello to my favourite sis (yes, I know, my only sis!).

Just spent two hot and dusty hours in the garage packing up the last of Matt's belongings. How could one man have so much pointless stuff? I hadn't realised he had so many sorts of boards (snow, surf, body, skate... I mean, a skateboard – really, a man of 38!), diving gear, rackets and clubs (assorted), climbing equipment and a kayak. With it all gone, I'm seriously thinking about selling the garage. I don't need it and the demand for parking in Pimlico is so high that they go for silly money, even without a house attached!

Looking at all this nonsense, I can't believe I was so blind to our hopeless incompatibility. What was I thinking? What a waste of ten years. I know they say opposites attract, but a city-trading adrenaline junkie with a love of gangster rap, and a hat maker who grew up wanting to marry Wilfred Owen (and we know that wouldn't have gone anywhere!!) – I think that was a step too far.

I hear on the grapevine that wife-number-two-in-waiting once played at junior Wimbledon, is in the county triathlon squad and, according to Matt, is very 'spiritual'. Apparently she's also tall, blonde and slim. Despite the fact that I hate her already, I hope they will be very happy together. ☹

Matt's brother Jon is going to pop around later to pick up the last few boxes, so luckily I won't need to see the rat - you know me, brave, hard face on the outside, quivering jelly on the inside.

Thanks for being a shoulder, I'm done with men! Love to Tom and the BFG.

Anna x

p.s. I've never asked but I hope Belle, Freddie and Georgia don't mind me calling them that – honestly, Izzy, what were you and Tom thinking, given what you, me and Robbie had to put up with when Mum signed our Christmas cards 'Love from Carole, Tony and the IRA'!!! Good job we never got raided by MI5 lol.

Email from Izzy to Anna

Hi little blister

Lovely to hear from you. The Rowbottom Rabble of Rockbeare are just dandy thanks.

Sod Matt the Ratt – granted, he was attractive in a rather obvious way, but he never deserved you. His new squeeze sounds horribly perfect or perfectly horrible, take your pick. I wonder if she is as vain as he is? Would love to be a fly on the wall while they bicker over one mirror in their bijou love nest! As she is thin and 'spiritual', from now on, I'll call her 'Miss Stick'.

I adore Tom but if he ever left me, I'd be over men too. Have you thought about getting a dog, or perhaps something more manageable like a goldfish?

Oh, and no, the kids don't mind you calling them the BFG. Belle says maybe some of my 'quirkiness' is rubbing off on you, which I thought was a bit rude. ☺

Lots of love

Izzy xx

p.s. I don't think your 'romance' would have got far with Wilf anyway, not because he was gay but because he was already dead!

Email from Anna to Izzy

Oh, I forgot to say, Gretchen comes from money. I think she has a penthouse or loft over in Islington somewhere, so sadly I'm sure they will have a huge designer bathroom mirror each.

Don't forget to write and tell me how your new job's going. Settling in?

Love

Anna xx

p.s. Mystic Miss Stick, love it!

Email from Izzy to Anna

Hey

Really enjoying the new job, thanks, although it's been a bit of a baptism of fire and it's very odd suddenly being one of the 'chosen ones' up on the Chief Officers' landing. Most of 'A' Shift wouldn't dream of setting foot on this hallowed carpeting by choice; the only time they would come up here is if they were being hauled over the coals by the Dep!

Just finished drafting the keynote speech for the Chief to give at the Superintendents' Association Dinner on Saturday night (Tom will be there but he's on strict instructions not to tell anyone I wrote it!) and am now frantically prepping for a fact-finding visit by a delegation of senior officers from Poland next week. You would be very proud that I'm learning the art of diplomacy and public relations. Oh, and I could get used to ringing up other departments and saying 'Hello, Sergeant Rowbottom from the Chief's office here' – amazing how quickly you can get stuff done. I hope the power doesn't go to my head.

After so many years, it's also quite nice working 9–5 and I get to travel into the office with Tom, which is a bonus. The kids are enjoying having a more normal routine too, and not having to creep around the house like when I was on night shifts.

I know my mates in local policing said the role of Staff Officer was just a glorified 'bag-carrier' but it's really testing all of my skills, most of which I didn't even know I possessed. I tell them it is much easier wrestling drunks in the gutter outside the Zodiac Lounge on a Saturday night lol!

Love

Izzy xx

BTW… what with this new broom or clean slate or whatever you call it (yeah, embracing the positives), I'm thinking about sponsoring a child at a school in Africa. A friend of a friend of one of my clients went to a posh lodge on the banks of the Zambezi for a holiday, where the owner set up a small school for her staff years ago that now caters for the whole district.

They are always looking for sponsors so I am going to do something good and worthwhile for a change. I love millinery but there's no denying it *is* a totally frivolous profession, so it would be nice to do something more fulfilling. Matt would have said 'charity starts at home' – which would have translated to 'can I buy a new kite surfer?' – but his needs are no longer my concern. Gosh, it feels quite liberating seeing that in print.

Speak soon.

Anna xx

Email from Izzy to Anna

That sounds interesting, let me know how it goes.

Email from Anna to Eleanor Alberon, Senior Manager, Anna Peel Millinery, Kings Road, Chelsea, London, SW3

Morning Ellie

I want to apologise for being a bit distracted lately – you know why. Sorry I've probably been boring you to death with all my woes but I think I am on the upward curve. Just have a few errands to run this morning and should be there about midday.

Before I get in, can you remind Leni there's a consignment of buckram due in any time, and can she ask Tris to take it over to the workshop if it arrives at the shop before I do? I think there is also a new set of blocks on order, but don't think they are due for delivery until later in the week. Also, Mark at the wholesalers mentioned he's had some really fine shocking pink sinamay just come in. It sounds like it could be ideal for Mrs Hardwicke's wedding hat – can you ask him for a sample?

I've checked the calendar and don't think I have any appointments until Wednesday so hopefully I can catch up before then. Thanks again, you have been a real star and I couldn't have got through the last few months without your support.

See you shortly.

Anna x

Email from Ellie to Anna

Hi Anna

No problem, boss.

I think Mark's just received a shipment from Italy of new felt as well, so will ask him for some samples at the same time. Also, do you want me to ask him if he can source some leopard-print netting? I'm not sure your formidable powers of persuasion worked with Lady Edgerton – she called earlier to insist it's still what she wants.

Hope okay, but I've popped an appointment for a private consultation in your calendar on Tuesday afternoon. I don't have a name yet, just a contact from an executive assistant. Seems the glitterati of Hollywood have woken up to your designs after Milan – I know it's an American actor but will be intrigued to see who she is. She must be an A-lister as I've been asked to close the shop thirty minutes before she and her entourage arrive. Again, hope okay?

Last on my list, you've had an invitation to visit André in Paris to discuss a new show he's creating for next year's New York Fashion Week. I think you're free early November so probably a good idea to firm this up now so we can get flights and hotels booked. If you can't fit in a visit to him, he says he's staying at the Lanesborough the last weekend of October so would love to treat you to dinner and a chat there.

Anyway, see you later and we can discuss further.

Welcome back!

Love Ellie x

✻

Email from Mr Kingsley Munyama to Anna

Dear Miss Peel

Thank you for your recent enquiry about our child sponsorship programme at Mwabonwa School. I am very pleased to provide you with further information as requested.

Our school was founded thirty years ago by Dr Samuel Nkomo and his wife Grace, who are the owners of Baobab Tree Lodge, which is located adjacent to our premises.

We currently have just over two hundred children from the wider Livingstone District, ranging from three years of age in our 'Tiny Tots' Reception class to our Year 12 students, who sit their Zambian School Certificate examinations before moving on to work or higher education.

Alongside myself and my deputy head teacher, Muchindu Tembo, we have fourteen teachers and other academic staff across a variety of departments, including science and maths, the humanities, sport and arts. Our staff also includes two administrators, one fundraising officer and a sponsorship co-ordinator and we supplement our teaching and support needs with a rolling programme of volunteers from all around the world.

Our aim is to make all our children excellent ambassadors for Zambia and worthwhile and productive global citizens, so we teach a broad curriculum including core subjects such as English, maths, geography and the sciences, as well as subjects like African history and vocational classes such as housecraft and needlework. We also encourage our students to develop additional life skills through our full after-school activities programme, which includes our Chess Club, the Girls' Empowerment Society, our Performing Arts Circle and our Junior Engineers, Technicians and Scientists (JETS) Club.

We couldn't do any of this most excellent work without our sponsors, so if you do choose to join us, your valuable contribution will help ensure we can continue to teach the children in the future.

I do hope this information has been useful to you. I look forward to you joining our programme shortly, when we will match your application with one of our students who is currently awaiting sponsorship.

Yours with most sincerity.
Kingsley Munyama Esq.
Head Teacher
Mwabonwa School
Post Bag 102
Livingstone
Zambia

Email from Anna to Mr Munyama

Dear Mr Munyama

Many thanks for the information you forwarded to me. Your commitment to the education and development of all the children in your care is very clear to see, and I have no hesitation in attaching my application form here.

I very much look forward to hearing from you in the near future.

Yours sincerely
Anna Peel (Miss)

Email from Mr Munyama to Anna

Dear Miss Peel

Thank you for joining our pupil sponsorship programme.

I am very pleased to write to inform you that we have matched your application with our pupil HENRY SISSONGA.

Henry is ten years of age. He likes English, history and geography, as well as playing football. His current career aspiration is to be an explorer, although the school would prefer it if he went into a more stable career such as teaching.

I will ask Henry to write to you to introduce himself more formally.

Thank you once again. Having committed sponsors like you is vital in ensuring the pupils here at Mwabonwa School flourish and become good citizens for Zambia.

Yours with most sincerity.

Kingsley Munyama Esq.

Head Teacher

Email from Mrs Grace Nkomo to Anna

Dear Miss Peel

I just wanted to drop you a short email to say thank you for signing up to our sponsorship programme at Mwabonwa School. I like to write personally to every new sponsor, as it really means the world to us all here to have regular and committed supporters onboard.

My husband Samuel and I founded Mwabonwa School for the twelve children of our staff when we opened Baobab Tree Lodge over thirty years ago and it has been the joy of my life to see it flourish and grow since then. Samuel sadly passed away last year, but he was so very proud of what we have achieved, as am I.

Thank you again, your support is greatly welcomed by all at Baobab Tree Lodge and Mwabonwa School.

Yours sincerely

Grace Nkomo (Mrs)

Owner Proprietor, Baobab Tree Lodge, Livingstone and founder of Mwabonwa School

Email from Anna to Grace Nkomo

Dear Mrs Nkomo

Thank you so much for your kind email, I am thrilled to be sponsoring a child at Mwabonwa School. I received an email from the Head Teacher, Mr Munyama, earlier today who says I have been paired with a little boy called Henry Sissonga. I hope to be writing to him soon.

I have been looking at your website and the Lodge looks beautiful. I would love to hear more about how you came to set it up, and the school too, but only if you have time to write again. It sounds fascinating.

Oh, and please, do call me Anna.

Kindest regards

Anna

Letter from Henry Sissonga to Anna

Henry Sissonga
Unit 5
c/o Baobab Tree Lodge
Post Bag 108
Livingstone
Zambia

Dear Miss Anna Peel

THANK YOU THANK YOU THANK YOU

My Head Teacher Mr Munyama has told my mother and father that you are now my sponsor, so I am writing to introduce myself to you.

My name is Henry Sissonga. I am ten and a half years of age and live with my family at Baobab Tree Lodge and go to Mwabonwa School. I am in Year Three class at primary level. My daddy, who is called Harold, is the head gardener at Baobab Tree Lodge. We live near the city of Livingstone which is close to our famous waterfalls. You call them Victoria but we call them Mosi-oa-Tunya, which means 'the smoke that thunders'.

I live with my daddy, my mother who is called Hester, my twin baby sisters, and my cousins who are also twins, Mabel and Milimo. They are sixteen.

Mr Munyama said I could send you an email as we have an IT room here at the school with ten computers. It is mostly used by the older children but other pupils are allowed to use it with special permission for urgent messages. However, I said I would like to write to you. One of my favourite lessons is English but I only got a 'C' grade for 'Penmanship' on my last report card. My year teacher Miss Banda wrote 'needs application' so I am hoping to improve this to a 'B' next term with more practice.

As part of my English Comprehension and Development class, I am also choosing a new word to learn every day. Today I have chosen PRECOCIOUS – do you know it?

I heard Mr Munyama say to my daddy that I am 'thankfully still on the right side of being precocious'. I asked Mr Nkosi, our librarian, what it means. He took down the big dictionary and says it means 'showing early or advanced mental development', which I think is a very good thing. I am not sure then why my daddy didn't look happier?

I look forward to your letter and to hearing more about you. Do you have a word of the day?

With very best wishes

Henry
Age 10 ½

✻

Email from Grace to Anna

Dear Anna

Thank you for your kind words, I was most touched.

Henry Sissonga is a bright and inquisitive child. He has been waiting for a sponsor for a couple of years so I know he is very happy to have finally been matched with you. I spoke with his father, who is our marvellous head gardener here at the Lodge, and he says little Henry hasn't stopped dancing and jumping around since he found out.

Before Samuel died, he always said I should write a book about our experiences over the last thirty years. We've certainly had some interesting times. If you would be happy to be my sounding board, I would be pleased and proud to tell you about our history and how we began. I certainly have the luxury of more free time now compared to the early days, so perhaps this is the ideal opportunity for me to get my memories onto paper.

While I still dabble, and particularly love to meet and greet our guests, we have such an accomplished team of staff, including my wonderful manager Esther, that I sometimes think of myself now more like the figurehead on an old sailing vessel – leading the way but a bit creaky and static, while everyone else pulls up the sails, mops the decks and steers the ship.

Let me sit and think for a while so I can marshal my thoughts, and I will write again soon, perhaps with Chapter One, called 'The Beginning'.

Before ending for now, Mr Munyama said you put 'Milliner' as your profession on your application form. How terribly glamorous! Many, many years ago and long before we moved to Zambia, Samuel and I once went to the Durban July Handicap, which I think is probably equivalent to your Royal Ascot. I remember I had the most amazing hat – it was black and white with lots of red organza – and how stylish I felt, even though I also distinctly remember that the sight of two black people at such an old and prestigious social event certainly caused a stir. That seems like a lifetime ago and, thankfully, in different times. If I can find a photograph I will send you a copy.

I very much hope to hear from you again and I would love to see some of your hat designs. And, of course, if you do write, please call me Grace.

Kindest regards

Grace

Letter from Anna to Henry

Dear Henry

Anna's word of the day: MILLINER

It was lovely to hear from you, and please do call me Anna so that we can be real friends.

I am delighted to be your sponsor and I am very happy for you to write to me whenever you wish, and to practise your spelling, grammar and penmanship. I must say I think your handwriting is already very neat. My handwriting is not nearly as good as yours, so I hope you will forgive me typing this letter on my computer.

I am thirty-five years of age and live in London, which is our capital city. I was born in the town of Torquay in the county of Devon, which is nearly as far south and west as you can go on the map of England. Torquay was the birthplace of Dame Agatha Christie, the most famous detective story novelist in the world.

I have never had a word of the day before but will make sure I think of a new one every time I write to you. My word today is MILLINER – which is the name of the job that I do for a living. A milliner is a person who makes hats. I make hats that are quite fancy for many special occasions, such as weddings.

I have enclosed a photo of myself for you. I hope you like it. My big sister Izzy took it at a music festival in Hyde Park in London last year. I don't wear daisies in my hair as a general rule, but it is a happy picture, I hope you will agree.

I look forward to hearing more about your life in Zambia, which should give you lots of writing practice.

Love Anna

Letter from Henry to Anna

Dear Miss Anna

Henry's word of the day: FRECKLES
I liked the way you put your word of the day at the start of your letter, so I am going to do the same.

Thank you for your letter and for the photograph. I like your dotty face. My geography teacher Mr Huismann said they are called freckles. Mr Huismann comes from the Netherlands so he says freckles are quite common there, but not many people here in Zambia have them. Mr Huismann is my favourite teacher as one day I hope to be an explorer like David Livingstone, who our great and wonderful city is named after. Although some people now call it Maramba, my daddy says we should never fear the past and an intrepid man is an intrepid man, wherever he is from or whatever the colour of his skin.

I showed my mother your photo too. She said you are very pretty and she liked your green eyes. Mother said Mama Grace thinks I should ask Mr Huismann to write to you as his wife and child died, and she says Mama Grace thinks he has a lonely soul, but Daddy told her not to gossip. Mama Grace kindly gave me some drawing pins so I now have your photo on the wall next to my bed.

You asked me about my home so let me tell you more about it.

Our house is set behind the main lodge, alongside some of the other staff accommodation, down a short path from the kitchen garden where my daddy grows his fruit and vegetables. He is a most excellent cook. My mother says, 'Harold, I sometimes think you love those sweet potatoes more than you love me,' but I am sure she is only joking. He has lots of other different produce like okra, green beans and mangoes, and he is very proud of everything that grows. He says that God has blessed him and our land with great fertility, and that makes him proud to be a Zambian.

Our house is quite solid compared to some of the houses in the local village, which are made of mud bricks or wood and dried grass. It is made of breeze blocks with a corrugated tin roof and has a polished red cement floor and plastered walls. We are also lucky in that our house has its own electricity and a water standpipe that we share with only two other dwellings.

Some of our furniture came from the old lodge when Mama Grace wanted to buy new, including my daddy's big armchair, which only he is allowed to sit in after work. We call her Mama Grace because Daddy says God took her only child so she could be the mother to every child at the school.

We have four rooms: a living room, a bedroom for Daddy, Mother and the babies, a bedroom that my cousins share, and one for me. My daddy says it is important I have my own room as my cousins are now young ladies and need their privacy. We have an outside kitchen with a thatched roof and a small porch covered in shade-netting where my mother sits when it is really hot. She likes to rock the babies in their crib with her foot while she is sewing. My daddy made the crib from an old tree stump and decorated it with carved hippos, elephants and monkeys. It took him a long time, but he was very proud of it when he had finished and says one day I will be able to put my own babies in it. I have done a drawing of the crib for you. It is not very good but I hope you like it.

Love
Henry

❈

Dear Miss Peel

I hope you do not mind me emailing you without an introduction, but Miss Grace has told me you were asking about the history of Baobab Tree Lodge and our wonderful school, and she is going to write and tell you more about us.

Grace is so proud of the Lodge and the school, as we all are.

I have been with Grace since the very earliest days and have her to thank for all my happiness in life. I was newly widowed with a small child when she employed me as a secretary and administrator, and my daughter Agness was one of the first children to benefit from our little school. Agness eventually went to university in Lusaka to study chemistry and now works as a pharmaceutical scientist. She specialises in research to find a cure for malaria, which makes me very proud.

If Grace doesn't mention it, I would love you to ask her why we call her the 'Matchmaker of Maseru'. Grace was the first person to see that I liked our handyman George, and he liked me, even before we knew it ourselves. She just knows when two people are meant to be together and she must be right, as my darling husband and I have now been married for twenty-eight years and have been blessed with six children together, as well as my lovely Agness, and twelve grandchildren.

After you wrote, Grace asked our new handyman Thomas to get her old photograph albums down from the loft space above the Lodge and it made me very happy to see her sitting in what we call The Observatory – the covered porch next to the Zambezi – going through each box. There is a big comfortable sofa that fronts on to the river and it is a lovely spot when the heat of the day has lifted, the sun is setting over the river and the breeze drifts in across the water. Miss Grace found a photograph of her and Mr Samuel at the races. She has asked that I scan it and send it to you, so please find attached. Grace says sorry it is in black and white, but she hopes you can still see how beautiful her hat was.

I hope it is not too forward but, if you have time, I do hope you will write to Miss Grace again. She has not been herself since Mr Samuel died last year, but since she wrote to you, she has been quite the most animated and engaged I have seen her in many months, so we do hope you can find time to write.

With all very best wishes
Esther Ng'andu (Mrs)
Baobab Tree Lodge, General Manager

Email from Anna to Grace

Dear Grace

Thank you for your email, and for the photograph that Esther sent me. I must say, you and your husband made a very glamorous couple, and your hat was truly stunning.

I agree that some people would think being a milliner is a glamorous profession, but I must confess, I mostly find it very hard work. I hope you don't think it is inappropriate, but I have used the photograph to design a hat that is very similar to yours, which I will add to my spring collection. I have attached a copy of my sketch here for you to see as well as some others from my current portfolio, which you may be interested in. I usually create two collections each year on top of my bespoke work, which I find very enjoyable. I name all my hat designs so have decided to call this new hat 'Grace'. I hope you approve.

I look forward to hearing from you again when you next feel able to write and would of course love to hear more about how you set up the Lodge and how you came to found Mwabonwa school.

Also, Esther says you are sometimes called the 'Matchmaker of Maseru'. I am intrigued, do tell me more!

Kindest regards

Anna

Email from Grace to Anna

Dear Anna

Oh, how wonderful!! You are so talented. The design for the new hat looks stunning and I am so touched that you named it Grace. Samuel would have been tickled pink.

Pay no mind to my Esther, she is a good Christian woman with a strong faith but she hedges her bets – I think that is how you say it – with a generous splash of superstition, as is sometimes the Zambian way. She is also an unashamed romantic. I don't think she has ever been the same since she found a copy of *Wuthering Heights* in the school library.

It is true, I do seem to have a recurring habit of bringing people together, which gives me such pleasure, but I would never class myself as an official 'matchmaker'. I think it is mostly down to the beautiful, magical place we call home, perhaps helped on a little bit by me. I had forty wonderful years of marriage with Samuel, so perhaps I just want everyone to have such happiness.

Esther has been with me almost since the very beginning and I am sure she thinks I am some sort of witch (a nice one, I hope!) because she often says, 'Miss Grace, without you I would have been alone, but you used your magical powers for good when you brought me to George and George to me.'

I must confess that no magic whatsoever was used in bringing Esther and George together. I just like to think I am a good judge of people. When I saw how George looked at Esther... let's just say that his gaze lingered on her two or three seconds more than it should have, and with how kind he was to her daughter Agness, I just knew.

They never realised, but it was so easy to engineer times when they would have to be together... 'George, can you go to Reception and ask Esther for the latest figures on visitor numbers?' 'Esther, I am too tired to walk to the vegetable garden today, can you please take this bale of shade netting to George?'

Although it seemed to many like an odd match, I also like to think I was just as instrumental in bringing little Henry's parents, Harold and Hester, together. Harold was nearly forty years of age when he came to Baobab, having spent fifteen years working in gardens all around the world and mixing with people of all nations. He is an extremely interesting character and something of a philosopher and poet, and he and my Samuel were very close.

Hester was just twenty and already working as a maid here. I am not sure if anyone has told you, but she is incredibly beautiful, as the people from the very north of Zambia often are. She had a kind soul but was perhaps a little vain and immature, as girls can be at that age.

At first there seemed to be no spark between them. Harold thought of her as frivolous and shallow; Hester thought of him as old and dull. But I just knew they were right for each other. He gave her security and made her think more deeply. She brought out his less serious, more fun side. I eventually found out they both had a love for singing and encouraged them to start a Lodge choir, which we still have to this day.

Well, to cut a long story short, within a year they were married, and one year later, lovely little Henry was born. Just the other evening, the breeze was gently blowing from behind the house, as it often does at this time of year, and I could hear them, sitting, on their porch singing a traditional Bantu song in such beautiful harmony, which made me so very proud and happy to be African.

With best wishes

Grace

Letter from Anna to Henry

Dear Henry

Anna's word of the day: HEIRLOOM

Thank you for your letter and for the lovely drawing of the crib your father made. You are a very accomplished artist for someone so young.

I like to draw and make things too! I sent draft sketches of my hats to your Mama Grace and have designed a new hat especially named after her. I have never made anything out of wood, but I use lots of other materials in my work, like felt, straw, netting, feathers and silk.

Your father is obviously very talented to have created

such a wonderful family piece. My word of the day means something precious that you inherit and pass down through the generations.

Love

Anna x

Letter from Henry to Anna

Dear Miss Anna

Henry's word of the day: ENDANGERED

Thank you for saying my daddy is talented. I told him and he looked very pleased. He said 'heirloom' is a perfect word to describe the crib he made.

He doesn't have very much time to carve as he works long hours, and he says it all depends on if he can find any suitable wood on the ground. Daddy found the wood for the crib when he was in the bush with his friend Moses, who is a wildlife protection ranger in Mosi-oa-Tunya National Park and looks after a small group of white rhinos that are famous as they are the only ones in the whole of Zambia. It makes my daddy sad because poachers come along to try to kill them for their horns, but Moses and the other rangers do everything they can to keep them safe. Daddy says the word I have chosen today is a good one to describe the plight of many African animals today.

Love

Henry

✢

Dear Anna

As promised, here is Chapter One of my Zambian story.

I am originally from Lesotho, just north of the capital Maseru but, before we moved to Zambia, my husband Samuel and I lived in South Africa. I was working as an English teacher in Paarl near Cape Town and Samuel, who had a Doctorate in Applied Mathematics, was the headmaster of a school in Stellenbosch. His job gave us a certain social cachet and standing in the community but, as you can imagine, life was still quite challenging for us both, as black academics, in a society which at the time was working so hard to maintain the hierarchy.

Samuel's family was originally from Zimbabwe and he had spent many happy holidays as a child with his grandparents, who lived in the town of Victoria Falls, close to the Zambezi river – although obviously on the other side of the border from where we are now. His memories of the place were vivid. I often think that places we love as children get deep into our souls and live there forever. We both loved our work but our jobs were starting to leave us feeling unfulfilled and Samuel often half-joked about quitting academia and opening a small hotel on the banks of the Zambezi. I used to tease him that he was probably less interested in a second career in hospitality than he was in being able to spend his time fishing and birdwatching, two of his passions in life.

Well, when the old colonial lodge came up for sale we were in a bit of a quandary. At the time, land ownership was a complicated business which I won't bore you with, but it was very hard for non-Zambians to own land on the Zambian border, which is why we turned to my husband's dearest and oldest friend Joseph, who was the best man at our wedding, for help. Joseph was born and grew up in Livingstone and had known Samuel since they were both boys. At that time, Joseph was working as a landscape gardener and had a keen eye for native plants. Like my Samuel, Joseph is no longer with us, but we were all proud that, when he died, he owned one of the largest landscaping businesses in southern Zambia.

You could say we all took a leap of faith, and so went into partnership together. We pooled all the meagre savings we had, sold many of our personal possessions – I even pawned my engagement ring – and begged and borrowed from our families until we had scraped together the asking price, with enough left over we thought to allow us to do the necessary renovations and get us through the first year. We bought the lodge unseen, the twenty acres of bush it sits on, a two-mile stretch of Zambezi river frontage and a small unoccupied island about three miles upstream.

When we first got to see the lodge in person, it was a bit of a shock, particularly for Samuel. He always liked certainty and order, two very important qualities in a mathematician, I think you will agree. I have to confess we had a few wobbles then and some sleepless nights!

Although it had a wonderful position on the banks of the Zambezi and had once been a very grand residence, the Lodge had been abandoned and fallen into disrepair in the early 1960s and, in truth, it was little more than a collection of dilapidated buildings, stores and shacks. At that time the country was fighting hard for independence, and thinking of how to bring the awe-inspiring natural wonders of the Zambezi and the Falls to the wider world was not the most important thing occupying the minds of average Zambians. And that is how it all began.

I hope you won't mind but I will end my first chapter there. I confess I find it a bit tiring typing these days, and I have a group of Canadian visitors arriving in an hour or so who I would like to greet, as I always try to do.

I will write again and tell you more about the Lodge and our little island, and how we transformed it from the early days of tents, bucket showers and DIY latrines. The school is another story altogether and equally interesting, I hope you will agree.

Until I write next, with kindest regards,

Sincerely

Grace

Letter from Anna to Henry

Dear Henry

Anna's word of the day: BIODIVERSITY

Thank you for your letter. I was very sorry to hear about the plight of the rhinos in Zambia but your father obviously cares very much for the natural world, which is why I have chosen my word of the day for you. It means the enormous variety of life on Earth, working in perfect balance.

While writing, I hope you will accept this small gift from me. I know you will find the fountain pen very useful in improving your penmanship and I hope having your own dictionary will help when you are choosing your word of the day.

Mr Munyama told me you would like to be an explorer one day, so I have also included here a large map of the world for you to put up in your bedroom, and a box of colourful map pins for you to use – but keep them away from the babies.

Love

Anna

Letter from Henry to Anna

Dear Miss Anna

Henry's word of the day: CARTOPHILE

Thank you very much for the fountain pen and pocket dictionary. My daddy said you are very kind and generous and I agree, but Daddy hopes you won't spoil me as he is a great believer that work and application will bring their own rewards and mean no man should be beholden to another, so I have given the pen to my cousin Milimo. She is just about to sit her exams and it will help her writing. My daddy said that was a nice thing to do and he is sure you won't mind. She has said I can borrow it back when I want to write to you.

I was also very happy to receive the dictionary, which Daddy says I can keep. It isn't as big as the Oxford English Dictionary Mr Nkosi uses but that would be too heavy to carry every day, and the one you have sent me fits into my satchel with my pencils.

I am going to use my new dictionary to learn a new word every day, as we have a Spelling Tournament at school soon. Although it is only for pupils aged eleven and above, Miss

Banda says my English is better than the others in my year so it has been agreed I can take part. I was very excited when she told me but now I am a bit nervous.

My daddy very much liked the map you sent me, as he travelled the world before he returned to Zambia. He says if I want to be an explorer, I will have to love maps, so that is what my word of the day means.

He helped me put it up on my bedroom wall, alongside your photo and my flag of Zambia. My daddy says each colour in our flag has a special meaning, so we marked Livingstone with a green pin, which represents our natural world, and we marked my father's birthplace of Kitwe in orange. He says this represents the heart of our country's Copperbelt. I also marked London on the map of England. I was not sure what colour to use so have chosen blue. My mother held the twins up to see it. They don't understand what it is but they seemed to like the colours, but I did as you said and made sure they couldn't touch the pins.

Love

Henry

Letter from Anna to Henry

Dear Henry

Anna's word of the day: ALTRUISTIC

It was lovely to hear from you. I can't write a long letter today as I am catching a train later this morning to travel to Edinburgh, which is the capital of Scotland (is it on your map?), to meet a new supplier, but I did want to wish you all the luck in the spelling tournament.

And, of course, I don't mind at all that you have given the pen to Milimo, that was a very caring and unselfish thing to do, as your daddy says. Why don't you write and tell me more about her, and Mabel and your baby sisters too.

See my word of the day above which I chose specially to describe what you did. You can look it up in your new dictionary to see what it means.

Take care and write soon.

Love

Anna x

✿

Letter from Henry to Anna

Dear Miss Anna

Henry's word of the day: ENTREPRENEURIAL

I hope you are well. I am happy to tell you more about my family. It will help my writing.

My little sisters are called Hannah and Harriet. They are over one year old but not quite two. They aren't very interesting yet – they spend most of their time sleeping, gurgling and crawling after the chickens in our yard, even though daddy says, 'Hester, stop the girls annoying the birds or they will stop laying.'

Daddy says twins run in our family, and that it is a blessing from God when you have two babies at the same time. Milimo and Mabel are the daughters of Daddy's only brother John and his wife Mary, who both died when the girls were quite small. My father said the illness that took them has been cruel in Africa and many good people have gone to God before their time, so he took the girls into his care, which was the right and proper thing to do.

Milimo means 'one born to be hard-working' and we are all proud that she wants to be a doctor one day. Daddy says Mabel has more of an entrepreneurial spirit, which means she is just as clever as Milimo but in a different way. My mother says this is a very hard word to spell so it may come up in the spelling tournament. She is right – I keep getting the vowels muddled up.

Mabel is very talented with hair and braids and at the weekends she works at the 'Cut Above Beauty Parlour for Beautiful Women' in Livingstone as a hairdressing junior. After she finishes school, she would like to open her own salon and go to college in the evenings to learn beauty therapy, but it is very expensive so she is saving up all her money from the salon, and she also helps in Mama Grace's restaurant three evenings a week. She is already daydreaming about the name for her new salon, as I've seen her doodling on the cover of her homework book. At the moment she says she can't decide between 'Mabel's Braids and More' or 'Livingstone Lovely Hair and Beauty'. Which do you think is best?

Love
Henry

Letter from Anna to Henry

Dear Henry

Anna's word of the day for Henry: ALLITERATION

Thank you for your letter, and for telling me a little more about your family. I have an older brother and an older sister too, so Harriet and Hannah will look up to you when they grow up.

Does it get confusing that there are so many of you in your family with a name that starts with the letter H? (See my word of the day to you.) When my sister and I were about your age, we used to like silly sayings that we called 'tongue-twisters' because they all started with the same letter and were hard to say really fast. Ask Mabel or Milimo to say 'Peter Piper picked a piece of pickled pepper' or 'she sells seashells on the seashore' and see what I mean.

Love

Anna x

p.s. Tell Mabel I like 'Mabel's Braids and More'!

Letter from Henry to Anna

Dear Miss Anna

Henry's word of the day: INTRACTABLE

What does 'p.s.' mean? I couldn't find it in my dictionary.

Thank you for the tongue-twisters, we have all been trying to say them really fast. Mabel is the best at them, followed by my daddy and then me.

I showed my daddy your letter and he laughed out loud for five whole minutes and then read it to my mother because she speaks English but is not very good at reading it. He said, 'There Hester, Miss Anna is a sensible woman and you are a silly, stubborn woman. She is wise and level-headed because she agrees with me.'

When the babies came along, my mother and father had a big argument because Mother wanted to name them Hannah and Harriet, and Daddy said, 'Why does everyone in this family have to have a name starting with H? It will be so hard when they all grow up for us to know which is which and who is who. What happens when they get an important letter from the bank and it just says 'H Sissonga'? How will we know who it is for? I forbid it.'

My mother sulked for three days. She slammed the pots around in the kitchen, glared at the chickens when she was feeding them until they stopped laying, and scalded me for kicking my football against the wall and for not doing my homework. Before long, my daddy said, 'Alright Hester, you can call the twins Hannah and Harriet but definitely no more children called Helen, Hudson, Harvey, Hazel or Hector,' and my mother agreed. My daddy says if God blesses them with another child, it will be a boy and he will be called Samuel, after Mama Grace's husband, who my daddy loved and admired very much. I am called Henry after my daddy's daddy.

My mother says Daddy likes an easy life so she knew he would give in eventually. She had a huge smile on her face for days afterwards and spent a lot of time singing as she swept the floors and washed the clothes. My daddy tried to look angry but he couldn't keep it up for as long. He said my mother would have been in a bad mood until the girls went to college if he hadn't let her have her way.

My daddy gave me my word of the day. He said it perfectly describes my mother's stubbornness.

Love

Henry x

Dear Henry

Anna's word of the day: COMPROMISE

Thank you for your letter. It really made me smile and reminded me of a similar argument my own family had when I was born.

I am the baby of the family. My father wanted to call me Myfanwy (pronounced Ma-fan-wee), which is a Welsh name. His mother, my granny Glynnis, was born in Cardiff so was insistent that at least one of us children have a Welsh name. She had tried with my older brother and sister too, but my mother didn't like her suggestions of Carys or Daffyd, so stuck firm to her choices of Isabel and Robert.

When I was born, my mother wanted to call me Anna after her mother and was absolutely against calling me Myfanwy. She didn't want me to be nicknamed Fanny!

Like your mother and father, a bit of a disagreement took place but, after some negotiation, my mother eventually agreed to compromise. She said that I could be christened Angharad, which means 'much loved' in Welsh, but from the day she brought me home from the hospital, she insisted on calling me Anna. She said it was just a shortened version of Angharad anyway and much easier for my brother and sister, who were still little, to pronounce. So, ever since, I have been Anna, and no one has ever called me Angharad – except my granny Glynnis, who still refuses to call me Anna!

I can't help feeling that, like your mother, my own mother ended up with the upper hand even though it looked like she had been the one to compromise!

Love

Anna x

p.s. You also asked about p.s. This stands for the word 'postscript', which comes from the Latin word postscriptum, which literally means 'written after'. In the old days, when everyone wrote letters to each other, it was useful if you had forgotten to say something in your letter and wanted to add it on to the end, or if, like this letter, you wanted to introduce a new subject that didn't fit in with the theme of the main letter. If you need to add too many though, you probably need to start to write your letter from scratch.

Email from Grace to Anna

Dear Anna

After I wrote last, I sat down with my photograph albums. My memory isn't what it used to be but Esther reminded me about all the other people who have met here at Baobab and at Mwabonwa. She said, 'Miss Grace, you truly are the African Dolly Levi,' which I have to confess made me laugh out loud.

There have so been many others over the years. Our porter Akim and Charity who worked in Reception, now happily married and living in Lusaka with their three children. Mrs Dorothea Chanda and her husband Jackson met when they came to work here in the kitchen on the same day five years ago and have been married for four. Ella, our current Reception class teacher and Piet, our boatman and wildlife guide. Even George's new apprentice handyman Thomas is courting – although I think that is a word that may have gone out of fashion – a young local girl called Ruth who works in housekeeping, and they have only been with us for less than a year. Perhaps I am like Dolly Levi after all!

The only one I've failed with so far is our wonderful geography teacher Dann Huismann.

I am very fond of Dann – in truth, he is more like a son to me, and he was so good to Samuel last year when he was dying. After he'd finished teaching for the day, Dann would take Samuel out on the river. I would pack blankets, binoculars and Samuel's favourite book, *The Complete Compendium of the Birds of the Zambezi*, into the boat alongside a cool box full of beer. I wanted to disapprove but Samuel would take my hand and say, 'It doesn't matter now, Grace,' and Dann would take him down the river for an hour or two. Birdwatching was a true pleasure that Samuel never tired of, even after thirty years, and it brought him great peace and acceptance towards the end.

Dann has a kind soul and I think him quite handsome, although I am not sure everyone agrees with me. He is funny and actually quite shy, although you would never know it when you first meet him as he can sometimes be gruff and strict, as former military men often are.

Dann has had a lot of sadness in his life and was in a dark place when he came to Mwabonwa five years ago. I don't think I have told you yet but Samuel and I lost our only child, a daughter, Elisabeth, when she was four, and when he came to us, Dann had also just lost a child and also his wife Anika. I don't know if I could have borne it when my Elisabeth died if Samuel had not been with me to be my rock, and I know those are deep scars on Dann's heart that he will carry forever, even though he tries hard not to show it. I know Zambia has helped him heal but there is still some way to go.

Unfortunately, he is proving to be quite stubborn and has so far resisted my attempts to find him new love. I say, 'Dann, six years is a long time. You will never forget them, and you will never truly get over the death of your son, but I know your wife would want you to find happiness again,' but he just shrugs his shoulders and says he is fine on his own.

I did have a little bit of hope last year when a Danish academic called Dr Lottie Lund came to Mwabonwa to do some geological research on the Falls. I forget exactly, but she is some sort of specialist in tectonic plates I think, working in the Geosciences Department at Aarhus University. I know brains are far more attractive than beauty, and this sounds frivolous, but she is also very pretty as well as being so accomplished. She speaks four languages, almost as many as Dann – can you imagine such a thing?!

I thought she and Dann would make a perfect match. They had a lot in common and certainly made a very handsome couple, him being so dark and her so fair. I thought I did detect a spark between them. They seemed to spend a lot of time in each other's company and I even saw them kissing once, but before anything could develop, Lottie had to return to Denmark at the end of her research secondment.

Despite the fact I have not been successful so far, Esther says I am a determined and stubborn woman, so I will never give up hope. I see you call yourself Miss Peel – does that mean you are unmarried? If so, perhaps I will ask Dann to write to you. I think it would do him good.

Anyway, enough of my silly musings. Next time I write, I will tell you how we came to set up Mwabonwa. When I see it now, I am amazed at how far we have all come on this amazing journey from such humble beginnings.

Love
Grace

Letter from Henry to Anna

Dear Miss Anna

Henry's word of the day: COMPARTMENTALISATION
The Spelling Tournament is in two weeks' time, so I am spending a lot of time reading my dictionary and will write again after the competition to let you know how well I did. I have a small wind-up torch and have been revising under my bed covers at night, although I get shouted at by my mother if she catches me. She says I will end up with cross eyes. Does that mean they will be angry?

We've just had the rules we have to follow and one category is for words of sixteen letters or more. I didn't know any, and neither did my daddy, so I asked Mr Huismann. He came up with my word of the day – it has twenty letters! He says it is a word he learned a long time ago and it means putting physical items, thoughts or feelings into separate boxes so they don't mix. I said, 'Like gravy and custard?' ar he said, 'Something like that.' I like it!

I hope I win so I can choose something fro Teacher's prize table.

Love

Henry

Letter from Anna to Henry

Hello Henry

Anna's word of the day: CONVERSATIONALISTS
I couldn't do as well as Mr Huismann, but I have chosen a word that is eighteen letters long. It means people who are fond of engaging in conversation, so I think it is perfect for you and me.

When you next write, I hope it is with good news with regards to the spelling tournament. I am intrigued by Mr Munyama's special prize table, do tell me more!

Love

Anna

Letter from Henry to Anna

Dear Miss Anna

You asked about Mr Munyama's prize table. Every week, at assembly on Friday, Mr Munyama announces the best pupils for that week. There are prizes for Penmanship, Neatest Uniform, Diligence and Application, Good Deed of the Week, Being a True Zambian Neighbour and Most Improved.

The pupils who are the best in each category can go up to Mr Munyama's special table and choose a prize. Sometimes the table looks a bit bare and my mother says Mr

Munyama or Mr Tembo often have to go into Livingstone to buy some new prizes with their own money to make it look more appealing, otherwise the children who win more often than others moan that the prizes are always the same.

There are usually lots of things like small toys, pens, hair clips, model cars, games and books. Most of the girls like the hair bands and the boys like the toy cars, but I would like the stationery set that has been on the table for a long time. It has a ruler, an eraser and highlighter pens, as well as a small stapler and pencil sharpener. I have never been announced as the best pupil in any category, but I am working on improving in all areas so that one day I may be. I know that the winner of the Spelling Tournament is going to be allowed to choose two items from the table, which is a great honour.

Love

Henry x

Email from Anna to Izzy

Hey sis

I want to send a parcel to Zambia so the Head Teacher at the school can top up his prize gift table – I'll tell you more next time I write. Do the BFG have any small toys (not Barbie, nothing electronic, and preferably unused or at least clean, not chewed, covered in crayon etc!) they no longer want that I can fit into a shoe box? I am thinking hair bands, toy cars, games (small ones), stationery, books. Nothing too heavy – it's really expensive to send large parcels to Zambia.

Speak soon.

Anna xx

Hey

No problem, I will grab some bits and bobs and post them to you. Half of the stuff they own has never even been out of its packaging, I think it's called conspicuous consumption, or just being spoiled rotten by grandparents!

Love

Izzy xx

✻

Parcel and letter from Anna to Mr Munyama

Dear Mr Munyama

Greetings to all at Mwabonwa.

Henry has written to tell me about your Prize Table, so please do accept this box of items, which I hope will be suitable for the children.

Kindest regards

Anna Peel (Miss)

Email from Mr Munyama to Anna

Dear Miss Peel

Thank you for your very generous parcel. The children will be very happy that there are some new items on the Prize Table, which I have to confess was starting to look a little threadbare.

Yours with thanks and sincerity
Kingsley Munyama, Head Teacher

Letter from Henry to Anna

Dear Miss Anna

Henry's word of the day: TESSELLATION
My daddy says it is important to be positive in life, and that you should always put good news either side of bad news, so the good news is that Mr Munyama's special table now looks splendid with all the gifts you sent.

He told us in assembly on Friday that you had sent a shoe box of prizes for us to share, and he had never seen such an expert display of tessellation. I didn't know this word so looked it up in my dictionary. It means 'the art of arranging shapes so they fit closely together without gaps'.

The bad news is that I didn't win the Spelling Tournament, but I did come third, which everyone said was very commendable for a child of my age. We have been doing a project in history class this year on ancient Egypt, so I was disappointed in myself that I spelt 'pharaoh' wrong (I put the O and A the wrong way around). A boy called Mwiya

Mulenga won. He is the brother of our Head Girl, Beauty, and he is nearly sixteen and almost as clever as her, so I did feel proud I had got so far.

The good news is that, for the first time, I was named as the 'Most Improved' pupil this week, so I was allowed to choose a gift from Mr Munyama's table anyway. I was going to pick the stationery set for myself but Mabel had seen some brightly coloured combs she really wanted, to practise her hair designs, so I picked those for her instead. My daddy says this was the right thing to do as 'entrepreneurs' like Mabel don't often have their type of cleverness rewarded at school and I will have lots more opportunities to get a prize as long as I am diligent and apply myself to my studies. Daddy says Zambians always help those less fortunate than themselves.

Love

Henry x

Email from Anna to Grace

Dear Grace

Thank you for your email. I am sure you are teasing me about asking your Mr Huismann to write to me!

I did have to smile at the thought of you as Dolly Levi, though. My dad had a huge crush on Barbra Streisand, even though he denied it to my mum, and I must have seen *Hello Dolly* ten times when I was younger. Wasn't there a milliner in the film called Mrs Molloy who was tired of making hats and wanted a life of adventure?

There have been so many splendid matchmakers dotted

around in literature and films, you are in very good company. My personal favourite is Jane Austen's Emma Woodhouse, sometimes misguided and meddlesome but genuinely kind and, above all, a great believer in love.

Like Dolly and Emma, you certainly seem to have been successful in your matchmaking over the years, and I am sure, when he is happily settled, Mr Huismann will look back and appreciate your persistence and determination.

Kindest regards

Anna

Email from Grace to Anna

Dear Anna

I've borrowed a copy of *Emma* from our school library. When I was younger, I read *Pride and Prejudice* but Mr Nkosi says, in his view, this is a much finer, more nuanced work. I am looking forward to reading it very much.

On the walk back from the library, I passed Esther and said, 'Esther, from now on, you can call me Emma, not Dolly.' She looked so baffled, I laughed and sang all the way to the Lodge.

I will write again soon.

Kindest regards

Grace

Letter from Dann Huismann to Anna

Dear Miss Peel

Apologies for this unsolicited letter. Grace Nkomo and Henry Sissonga have insisted I write to you and won't stop pestering me until I have.

Henry says this is because, like his, my penmanship needs work, and you will give me an honest opinion. I suspect he is basing this fact on his report card, which even I struggle to read after I've written it, so I couldn't disagree with him. I suspect Grace has other motivations, but I don't mind indulging her this once.

Henry is a great kid, he is extremely bright and has a very enquiring mind, which means he sometimes (quite often!) has more questions than I can answer. You will enjoy your correspondence with him very much.

I have to say, he looked very determined when he came to see me this morning to say I should write to you. I suspect that was because Grace told him not to leave until I had. He even brought a new fountain pen with him that he said you had sent him to help with his writing. I know he gave it to his cousin but she has let him borrow it back to lend to me so that my writing is as neat as possible. It is certainly becoming a well-travelled pen! Given this level of determination and planning, I felt I couldn't refuse.

Henry says that when you write to someone for the first time, it is courteous that you tell them your age, where you come from, what you do for a living and what your hobbies are. He has obviously forgotten I'm not ten years of age, but here goes.

My name is Dann Huismann, and I am forty-two years of age. I was born and grew up in Maastricht, which is a very lovely university town on the river Maas, about two hundred kilometres south of Amsterdam. If I was writing a travelog, I'd also add that we have a lot of impressive medieval architecture, a cobbled old town and a vibrant culture, but I suspect you will know us only for that famous (infamous?) treaty! In terms of heritage, I am a bit of mongrel, I think you might say. My grandmother on my father's side was French, and my mother was actually born and grew up in America, but her late father was Dutch and her mother Portuguese.

I think Henry has told you that I am the geography teacher here at Mwabonwa. I would like to hope I am not as boring as that makes me sound, as I definitely don't own a tweed jacket with leather elbow patches – or perhaps that is just a childhood flashback to Mr Van Dijk from tenth grade?

I was a Captain in the Royal Netherlands Army for eight years before I retrained and have been teaching geography, with a smattering of geology, here for five years.

When not slaving over a map or some random rocks, I also run the chess club, repair the children's bicycles, coach the under-12s football team and, in my spare time, turn my hand to a bit of block-laying, as we are in the middle of building a new Women's Community Art Centre. Grace very kindly gifted the school a parcel of land from her grounds and, once open, we hope that the local village women will be able to learn more about sewing, textiles, and arts and crafts, so that they can set up their own businesses to help support their families. Like many of the local women, Henry's mother Hester is an excellent seamstress, so she is very excited.

I have shown Henry my letter to you. He has given me 8 out of 10 for my penmanship, and 7 out of 10 for content.

He didn't understand the bits about the geography teacher's jacket and the Maastricht Treaty but did like the fact I called him bright.

Thanks again for getting on board as a sponsor, we all appreciate it here and I know you will enjoy corresponding more with Henry.

Kind regards

Dann (Huismann)

Email from Anna to Dann

Dear Mr Huismann

Thank you for your letter – please let Henry know it arrived safely and I am happy to report back that I agree with his assessment of your penmanship and also give you 8 out of 10.

How exciting to be building a new arts centre especially for the local women. When do you hope it will be finished?

Kindest regards

Anna (Peel)

p.s. Despite my letter ending in a question, think of it as rhetorical and please don't feel you need to respond. I also suspect I know why Grace asked you to write to me. She has told me all about being the 'Matchmaker of Maseru' and I am planning on writing back to let her know that, while I appreciate the sentiment and good intentions, I would prefer her matchmaking gaze did not focus too closely on me. I fear, being in closer physical proximity to her, you are perhaps in more danger!

Email from Anna to Grace

Dear Grace

Although it was not necessary to ask him to do so, I am sure you would like to know that Mr Huismann has already written to me.

Grace, although I know you and I haven't been writing to each other for very long, I hope you aren't going to be mischievous and involve me in one of your matchmaking schemes. You are right that I am single but I can assure you I am perfectly happy on my own, now and for the foreseeable future.

Dann seems very nice but I don't imagine he will write again, or me to him. I am certain your talents and wishes for him would be better directed towards someone more suitable, more in need, and certainly closer to home.

While writing, please accept my sincerest apologies as it was remiss of me when I wrote last to say how very sorry I was to learn about your daughter Elisabeth. Losing a child must be the most terrible experience for any parent – I cannot imagine how awful it was for you and your husband.

Regards
Anna

Email from Grace to Anna

Dearest Anna

I am glad Dann has written to you. Does the fact that he is charming come across in his letter?

Thank you for your kind words about Elisabeth. Would it be alright if I digress from my tale of the Lodge and school to tell you about her? I ask because I rarely speak of her now, and not at all since Samuel's passing. Everyone here is very kind, but I think they worry that I will just cause myself too much pain by speaking about her.

I would love to tell you a little bit about her. She was a beautiful, fearless and wonderful daughter and a true blessing from God.

Kindest regards

Grace

Email from Anna to Grace

Dear Grace

As long as you are sure it won't upset you, I would love to know more about Elisabeth.

Kind regards

Anna

Email from Grace to Anna

Dearest Anna

I hope you like the photo I've attached, although the scan is a bit grainy. We didn't have camera phones back then, of course. It is of me and Samuel and Elisabeth when she was eighteen months old, on the day she was christened. Do you like her dress? I made it out of the lace from my own wedding dress, which used to be a popular thing to do. I still have it wrapped up tightly in a box of tissue paper in my wardrobe, but I rarely get it out to look at it as I know that would be too painful.

Having Elisabeth certainly wasn't planned and Samuel and I were, back then, what would be considered quite old parents – I was nearly forty and Samuel was ten years older – although I know that is now quite common. We had been married for twelve years and, while we had talked about having a family every now and then, it had just never happened and we had reconciled ourselves to being childless.

However, don't they say that the best way to conceive is to stop thinking about it? After we came to the Lodge, our first year was so hectic with all the rebuilding and the school, we hardly had time to draw breath – although after Elisabeth was born, Samuel used to tease me that we obviously had time to do other things – so when I found out I was pregnant, it was quite a shock.

I kept working at the Lodge even when I was nearly full-term, although I have to admit full days of painting, weeding and yard work in the heat of the dry season did start to take their toll on me. I was healthy but remember being huge and quite fractious by then, and my darling Samuel often bore the brunt of my mood, even though he never complained.

When Elisabeth was born, she was just the happiest, most content baby in the world. The local women taught me how to make a fabric sling to strap her on my back, so she went everywhere with me. Sometimes I even forgot she was back there until she was hungry and would fuss and grab my hair. There were many days when I was working that I would put her in her small playpen on the back porch of the Lodge, under the shade of an umbrella tree, and she would just sit and play with her toes all day long.

When she got a little older, Samuel and Joseph used to take her on bush walks. She would sit high up on Samuel's shoulders and he would point out all the birds, animals and plants and name them in English, and Joseph would then name them in the local dialect. I am sure she would have been a great naturalist and protector of Africa like her father and Joseph if she had lived.

Sadly, that wasn't to be. One day in April, when she wasn't quite five, she was listless and sleepy and a bit flushed. It had been very wet that year, and I thought she just had a summer chill, but later that day,she was hot to the touch and had a blotchy rash on her tummy. When she said, 'Mummy, the light is hurting my eyes' I got really scared, so Joseph got in our truck and drove as fast as he could to Livingstone for the doctor. Dr Mbele was a wonderful and caring man, and was our family doctor for over twenty years, but it took them nearly three hours to get back as the heavy rain had caused a landslide at the intersection near town, and a tree had fallen and blocked the road. By the time they arrived at Baobab, Elisabeth had already gone.

I was in such a state of shock, Samuel and Dr Mbele had to prise her body out of my arms. They said later she had had a virus, which turned out to be meningitis. I never really forgave myself, although Dr Mbele said there would have been very little we could have done. Even if she had reached the hospital earlier in the day, it was then small and very poorly equipped, and meningitis is such a rapid killer.

I don't think I cried for several weeks. Poor Samuel was my absolute rock, although I know how devastated he was too. We threw ourselves into our work, but sadly, God didn't bless us with any more children. I sometimes wonder if that is why the school meant so much to us over the years. We have been mother and father to hundreds of children and that does give me peace and purpose.

I have cried a little while writing, but it does feel good to speak about Elisabeth. I hope my letter hasn't made you sad. Looking back, what I feel most of all is that we were truly blessed, and I am sure God had a purpose for calling her home so soon, which I do not question.

With love, and thank you for letting me share my story,
Grace x

Email from Anna to Grace

Dear Grace

Elisabeth was a beautiful child and obviously a wonderful daughter, so I feel very privileged that you felt you were able to share her story with me. Thank you.

Love
Anna x

✤

Letter from Henry to Anna

Dear Miss Anna

Henry's word of the day: HIRSUTE
I asked Mama Grace if she would take a photograph for me

to send to you. She has a phone with a camera and she asked Esther to print it off in the Lodge office. I have tried to fold it neatly so none of the creases go across the faces. Perhaps you can put it on your bedroom wall? Mama Grace said it is important to write the date and names on the back of the photographs we take, as years later we may have forgotten who the people are. I told her I will never forget. She gave me a big smile and a hug but she looked a bit sad.

From left to right are my daddy, my mother holding the twins, Milimo, Mabel, me, Mama Grace and Mr Huismann.

Mr Huismann said it wasn't appropriate for him to be in the photograph, but Mama Grace was insistent. She teased him that you wouldn't be able to see his nice face through his big beard, but she says you can still see his kind eyes, so that will have to do for now. My daddy says Mr Huismann is 'hirsute', which I have chosen as my word of the day. It is just a funny-sounding word for having a hairy face.

I hope you like it.

Love Henry

Email from Anna to Izzy

Hey Iz

Hope all well with you – just thought you would like to see a photo of Henry and his family, which I've scanned and attached. Lovely, eh?

Email from Izzy to Anna

Hey back

Who's that tall guy on the right with the beard?
    Izzy x

That's Dann Huismann, Henry's favourite teacher.

Um, dishy!!

Can't say I'd noticed.

Really? 😊

Well, he has a nice smile.

He certainly has. I'm not keen on all that facial hair but I like his arms as well, they look very strong.

Izzy, I think we're in danger of going down some surreal

conversational rabbit hole here! Forget Dann Huismann's arms – what about Henry and his family?

Email from Izzy to Anna

Oh yes, sorry, inappropriately distracted for a moment.

Yes, little Henry's a real cutie isn't he. I think he's what Gran would have called a bobby dazzler. Attractive family too – especially his mum, she's absolutely stunning.

Love Izzy x

p.s anyway, young lady, I may be ancient (I certainly feel it some days) but there's absolutely nothing wrong with my eyesight. I can still appreciate a hot guy when I see one!

October

Email from Dann to Anna

Hello again Anna

Hopefully you don't mind me emailing you back – it is quicker than writing longhand, and I think I have now satisfied Henry's desire to improving my penmanship.

Please don't worry about Grace. I have had many years practice of resisting her misguided but good-intentioned matchmaking and, so far, I've always managed to stay one step ahead of her. I am confident I can do so again now in writing to you without either of us being in peril but, to be on the safe side, I won't tell her if you won't.

Anyway, I thought you might be genuinely interested in the Arts Centre – you did ask, after all, rhetorically or not! It's an important project locally and everyone I speak to in the surrounding area is very excited about it. We are about halfway through building the structure and we're just trying to get the walls finished so we can put the roof up before the rains come in November. I'm not sure if you have ever been to Zambia but, when it rains here, it really rains!

There is a team of about ten labourers. I am not officially one of them, of course, and they are much quicker and more proficient at block work than I will ever be, but I like to help out after classes have finished and I have also got quite proficient at cement work and plastering as well. I must remember to add these to my CV in case I ever fancy a change of career.

I do worry that now we have corresponded more than once, that means we are officially pen-pals? If so, and as I had to do the same on Henry's express instructions, you should tell me your age, where you come from, what you do for a living and your hobbies.

Best,

Dann

Letter from Henry to Anna

Dear Miss Anna

Henry's word of the day: OPHIDIOPHOBIA
We had a very interesting day in school yesterday, so I thought you would like to hear about it.

Do you like snakes? Daddy says Zambia alone has nearly one hundred different types of snakes. Most are harmless, but some of them are very dangerous. We learn about snakes when we are very little, and every year the youngest children do a project at school to draw the snakes that live in our part of Zambia. They hang their paintings around the classroom so they can learn which snakes are friendly and which are not.

Even though some are dangerous to humans, we learn

that all snakes are good because they eat the mice and rats that sometimes get into our houses and nibble at the sacks of soya or corn, and that snakes will only bite if we disturb them but that we have to be vigilant, especially when we are playing in the scrub or around trees.

On Wednesday in assembly, Mr Munyama said that the next day the whole school would be allowed to leave lessons early as a special team was coming all the way from Lusaka and were bringing some real live snakes to show us. He handed out some cards they had printed. They said:

Snakes Alive!

HISS – Helping Identify Snakes Safely

We were very excited. We have seen pictures of snakes in books but not many of us have seen one in the wild, although Mama Grace told us that they found a venomous twig snake at the Lodge last year, which Piet the wildlife guide captured and released into the bush before any of the guests saw it!

. When she told Daddy, she said she hadn't lost a guest in thirty years and wasn't about to start now.

On Thursday, the whole school gathered in our outdoor theatre. It is semi-circular and made of concrete tiers, with a stage at the front. We use it for our school plays and dancing competitions. Mr Tembo says there were many such structures in Ancient Rome and its proper name is an 'amphitheatre'.

On the stage, someone had set up two tables from the refectory, and on each table there were three glass tanks, each covered with a piece of cloth. There was also a board with a large poster pinned to it – it said 'Dangerous Snakes of Zambia, Protecting People and Snakes through Education since 1999'. The poster had twelve photos of the deadliest snakes on it, and information about danger levels and snakebite procedures. There was a lot of excitement and chatter around the theatre, and my heart was pounding a bit.

A young man who said his name was Ben and a young lady called Joanna, from Snakes Alive!, stood at the front of the stage and talked to us about the most deadly snakes in Zambia and what to do if we found one – move very slowly away and call for a teacher, and never pick up a snake or try to touch it.

Ben said some people have an overwhelming fear of snakes, so see my word of the day, which Ben had written on the blackboard. I copied it down as carefully as I could so I hope it is right. But as Africans, we value all snakes and want to protect them.

Joanna uncovered each glass tank one at a time and walked up through the amphitheatre to show us each snake as Ben told us a bit more about it. The first boxes had our most dangerous snakes. They are the Black Mamba, the Black-Necked Spitting Cobra, the Boomslang and the Vine Snake. I was a bit scared of the Black Mamba. Ben said this is the most dangerous snake in Zambia. It lives on the ground and in the trees, but he called it 'skittish and unpredictable' which can make it more dangerous than other snakes. I hope I never see one here!

My favourite snake was the Boomslang. It was not very big but it was beautiful, with an emerald green tummy and black stripes. It lives in the trees and often hangs down from the branches waiting to lunge at birds, lizards, small mammals and even other snakes. Ben said the Boomslang is also very deadly so we must be extra careful when we are running under low trees.

When the dangerous snakes were back under cover, we were allowed to go up in year groups to hold the last two snakes, a Common Wolf Snake and a Spotted Bush Snake, both of which are harmless. I thought they would be slimy but they were very dry to touch. I didn't want to hold one but I did stroke the Bush Snake, and some of the older children were braver than me and were allowed to handle them.

Ben and Joanna gave Mr Munyama several copies of the poster, and he said he will put up one in the refectory, one in the library and one in each year room, and that we should study them so we never hurt a snake in future, or let it hurt us.

Do you have any deadly snakes in England? Daddy says he doesn't think so, he says the climate is too cold.

I have to end my letter now as I still have some maths homework to do. I am not very good at maths, and I have to solve five long-division sums before my lesson tomorrow.

I hope you will write again soon.

Love Henry x

Letter from Anna to Henry

Dear Henry

Anna's word of the day: ECTOTHERMIC
What a fascinating experience you had with the snakes. I do not generally have a fear of snakes, but I think I would be very scared if I came across one of the venomous ones you have there in Zambia! We do not have any deadly snakes in England – in fact, we only have four native snakes and only one, the adder, can give you a nasty bite, but it is rarely fatal to humans.

Your daddy is right, it is too cold here for most snakes. See my word of the day for you to look up in your dictionary.

Like your snakes in Zambia, our snakes here are shy and elusive so I don't imagine I will ever see one in the wild.

I hope it is alright, but I have shared your letter with my niece Belle. She is about your age and loves all sorts of wildlife, even the things that slither and crawl about, so I know she will find it very interesting.

Love

Anna x

Email from Anna to Dann

Hi Dann

The new Arts Centre does sound amazing. How good of the school to think about the wider community and the empowerment of the local women.

No, I have never been to Zambia. I went to Cape Town once on a buying trip, which I enjoyed very much, but I would love to see more of Africa one day.

Anna

p.s. Aren't we a bit old to be pen-pals?

Email from Dann to Anna

Dear Anna

Henry showed me your photo (I liked the daisies by the way). I reckon we have at least seventy years between us, so perhaps!

Joking aside, and despite the fact that we are now partners in crime in relation to one of Grace's schemes, please don't feel obliged to write again.

Best, Dann

Email from Anna to Dann

Hi Dann

Lol – at least you didn't say we had a combined age of a hundred, otherwise I would have been offended.

Actually, it could be fun having a new pen-pal. I had a few when I was about Henry's age – before email, of course – but obviously none since then. Let me see if I can remember the format of the first letter. Here goes.

My name is Angharad Louise Peel, although everyone has always called me Anna, except my granny Glynnis, but that's perhaps a story for another day. I am thirty-five and was born in Torquay in Devon, in the south-west of England. Interesting fact – it is the only English county with two separate coastlines. In keeping with your travelog about Maastricht, Torquay is part of a coastal area called the English Riviera, so named by Victorian visitors who likened it to the south of France. It's in a beautiful and sheltered bay with sparkling water (when it isn't raining) and a distinct micro-climate – we have palm trees, you know!

I'm a milliner by trade. I moved to London to study when I was eighteen and opened my own design studio and shop in 2015. I make elaborate and very expensive bespoke hats for rich women, titled women, minor royals, WAGs and other largely vacuous wannabe celebrities.

In my spare time, I like history, reading and growing things, although strictly in pots, as I only have a tiny balcony in my flat. I have a mum and dad, brother, sister and brother-in-law (who are, or were, all police officers – more later, perhaps), two nieces, a nephew and an ex-husband, no children, no pets.

Grace is telling me all about how she and her husband came to open the Lodge and is going to write to me about the earliest days of the school too. She sounds like an utterly fascinating and determined woman, so I am not sure a geography teacher will be able to top that in the correspondence stakes!

Regards, Anna

Email from Grace to Anna

Dear Anna

I promised last time I wrote to tell you how Samuel and I came to set up the school. Perhaps this should be Chapter Two of my memoirs?

Being educators and passionate believers in the benefits of all children getting a proper education, when Samuel and I came to Zambia we also had some fanciful notion that we would be able to teach the children of our staff at the same time as start our new business. Of course, it didn't turn out that way – does anything in life? We were so busy with the building work and renovations (which I'll write and tell you more about at another time), we soon realised our dream of teaching the children ourselves was just that: a lovely dream but not remotely feasible or, frankly, achievable. We were still committed to the idea of teaching the children, so 'in for a penny, in for a pound' we thought, and decided to create a small separate schoolroom on our property and employ a local teacher.

A little distance behind the main lodge, we came across a dilapidated farm building, which we think had once been used to house pigs. When the school moved into the larger purpose-built premises it occupies today, we converted the old schoolroom into three dwellings for some of our staff – and in fact, Henry and his family now live in one of those properties.

The building was in a wild patch of native scrub and almost swamped by tangled thorn trees, but after spending a month of back-breaking work clearing the area and repairing the tin roof, we had ourselves a proper classroom.

It was very basic, of course. There were no windows, just openings in the wall, but I made some pretty curtains out of fabric I found at Mukuni Market to help keep the mosquitoes out and provide shade in the afternoon, and Samuel bought some broken desks and an old blackboard from an elementary school in Kazungula, which he and Joseph were able to repair. We were certainly 'Jacks of all trade' back then, and never was that old saying more true – necessity really is the mother of invention.

It was completely unnecessary, of course, but I also wanted to give our little school a proper name as I felt it would give the children pride, even though we only had twelve pupils in total. We eventually decided on Mwabonwa, which means 'Welcome'.

When the new schoolhouse was ready, I swept a dirt path leading from the back of the main Lodge buildings to the entrance, which I lined with large stones painted red, black, orange and green, which are the colours of the Zambian flag. On a post at the head of the path, I put up a sign saying 'Mwabonwa School at Baobab Tree Lodge'.

So, the only thing we were missing was a teacher.

I put an advert in the local paper, the Livingstone Daily Post and Herald, and three days later we received a letter from Mr Kennedy Matete.

Mr Matete told us he was seventy-two years of age and he had been a teacher at schools across Livingstone for fifty years but had been made to leave his last job because he had a neurological condition that meant he sometimes found it difficult to hold the chalk and occasionally had such bad tremors in his legs that he found standing for long hours too difficult.

We asked him to come along for an interview. In truth, he was the only applicant, but we wanted to do things properly. Later that week, he arrived at the property.

Despite it being the height of summer, and easily 35°c in the shade, Mr Matete had cycled all the way from Livingstone – no mean feat, given that it is about ten miles and at the time the main road was not tarmacked liked it is now, and our Lodge was, and still is, down another two miles of rutted dirt track – and he was wearing a three-piece suit with a blue bow tie, polished brogues and a trilby.

He also brought with him his dog Peter, a slightly raggedy lurcher crossbreed with only one eye, which had run alongside him the whole way. Despite his somewhat unprepossessing appearance, Peter later proved himself to be a loyal companion to Mr Matete and protector of the children, as well as an excellent snake dog.

To cut a very long story short, we hired Mr Matete and we never looked back.

He did occasionally have to sit down to teach when his legs shook, but he was wonderfully adaptable. If he was having a bad episode he would put down his chalk, pull up a chair and say, 'Today, children, I will tell you about my time in the Zambian resistance,' or 'Today, children, I will tell you how I once had a lion cub as a pet,' or 'Today, children, I will tell you how I survived going over Mosi-oa-Tunya in a canoe'. He was such a wonderful storyteller that the children didn't care whether his tales were true or not. The first two were but not the last one, as I am sure you can imagine.

Mr Kennedy Matete stayed with us as our first teacher, and latterly Head Teacher, for fifteen years until he sadly passed away. Having lost his wife forty years before, and several children in infancy, he had no family of his own, so we scattered his ashes up under our big baobab tree.

Last year, I scattered my darling Samuel's ashes up under the baobab too, as we had done with Elisabeth thirty years ago. There are no markers and no gravestones. Our tree is a living marker that could live for another thousand years, which is by far the best memorial we could ever have. Samuel was very proud to be the son of African soil, so his last wish was to return home.

When he was alive, there was nothing Samuel liked more than to sit up under the baobab with Joseph and Mr Matete on a cool evening, discussing politics or astronomy and drinking rooibos tea. I often wonder if his spirit is still sitting out there each night, looking at the endless black sky and infinite stars above Zambia, with Elisabeth snuggled up in his lap. I truly like to think so.

If I forget, remind me to tell you more about our beloved tree and the significance of the baobab to Zambia and across all of Africa.

Love

Grace

Letter from Henry to Anna

Dear Miss Anna

Henry's Word of the Day: ERUDITION

I saw Mama Grace yesterday and she said she has been writing to tell you about how she and Mr Samuel came to open our school. It was so long ago, it was before even my mother was born! She said it would be nice if I would tell you about our school now so I said I would write.

Mwabonwa is a great school. There are over two hundred pupils, and they come from all over the district. I am lucky that I live next door, but my best friend Boston Chibale lives in a village about five miles away and has to cycle here and back every day. When it is raining, he is often soaking wet by the time he gets to school and Betty in the office lets him hang his jumper out of her window to dry under the eaves. The track gets so muddy he often has to stop on the way to scrape out his bicycle wheels.

Our school is divided into four houses, each with a different colour representing the Zambian flag and all named after rivers. I am in Zambezi house, which is green. There is also Chongwe, which is black, Luwombwa, which is orange, and Mbereshi, which is red. We have a Head Girl and a Head Boy, they are called Beauty Mulenga and

Emmanuel Phiri. They are very important as they make sure all the children are in lessons and scald us a bit if we are late. Emmanuel is due to go to university in Lusaka to study journalism, and Beauty wants to go to Mulungushi University to study accountancy and international relations. They are both very clever. When I am older I would like to be Head Boy, but you have to be bright enough to go to university, and I may not have time if I want to be an explorer.

The littlest children at Mwabonwa are only three or four years of age. They do not do proper lessons, but they spend a lot of time painting, making shapes out of coloured paper and getting glue everywhere, singing, and sleeping each afternoon on mats under the shade trees. When you get to the age of six, you have a proper timetable showing all your lessons for the week. My favourite lessons are geography and English, but I also like history. I am not very good at maths but I do try hard.

We have eight large classrooms built around a central playground and with a small toilet block, water standpipe and our refectory just to one side. Every day, all the children get a piece of fruit at breakfast and a plastic cup of mealie meal porridge and vegetables for lunch as we have a food programme called 'Full Tummy, Full Brain'.

We also have a small library, an IT room and our amphitheatre, where we hold our morning assemblies, put on plays and have singing and dancing performances. Mr Munyama and Mr Tembo share an office, there is one for the administration staff, and a room with a kettle and comfy chairs where only teachers are allowed.

After school, I play in the under-12s football team, which

Mr Huismann coaches, and I would like to join the chess club when I am older. My daddy tried to teach me how to play last year but I found it very hard – there are so many different pieces that can all move in different ways. He said I am maybe a bit too young, so he will try to teach me again next year.

Do you like my word of the day? It means showing great knowledge or learning, so I think it is a good word to choose to describe our school.

Love

Henry

Letter from Anna to Henry

Dear Henry

Anna's word of the day: STRATEGISATION

Thank you for telling me all about your wonderful school.

I hope you do learn to play chess, it is a fascinating game. My dad taught me when I was just about a year older than you and I hope I can teach my niece Belle to play soon, as it will be nice to pass this knowledge down through the family. It can be a hard game to master but I hope you will persevere as it is well worth it.

I've chosen my word for the day, which describes something you need to excel at to be a good chess player.

Love

Anna

Hi Anna

Thank you for your email. I showed Henry and he said you also told him that Dame Agatha Christie was born in Torquay, so he is currently reading *The Secret of Chimneys*, which he got from the school library. Mr Nkosi keeps a shelf of mostly tattered old paperbacks that are left behind by Lodge visitors and which are picked up by the staff to read when they have some free time. I don't have a lot of the latter but, when I do, I am currently working my way through his large collection of Jo Nesbo's books.

I am really pleased you are writing to Grace, and totally agree with your assessment, including her relative merit compared to a humble geography teacher. While I am unremarkable, she is truly remarkable. Her husband Samuel was also an incredible humanitarian, academic and visionary. It has been a bit subdued around here since he died last year, so I am sure Grace will want to tell you everything she can about the early days as that seems to bring her some comfort.

Ending now, off to teach a class of fifteen-year-olds about river erosion and the formation of oxbow lakes. I can almost hear you saying, 'Wow, Dann Huismann, what a rock and roll life you lead!'

Best, Dann
p.s. WAGs??

Email from Anna to Dann

Dann

WAGS = British acronym common with the tabloid press, meaning 'Wives and Girlfriends', usually of high-profile top-flight footballers. Not always used in an overly complimentary way as it tends to describe a homogeneous group of young ladies, usually with long blonde hair and perfect tans, who have a liking for teeth whitening and plastic nips and tucks. I expect the Dutch press is far too egalitarian to use such a term.

Regards, Anna

p.s. I'm in no position to make fun of geography teachers... True and embarrassing story, which shows you what a terrible big sister I had – when I was young, she convinced me that a Volcanologist was someone who studied Star Trek! Does that translate from English into Dutch?

p.p.s. I also love a bit of Scandi crime fiction.

Email from Dann to Anna

Anna

In the Netherlands, we call them VEVs (Vrouwen en Vriendinnen).

Dann

Email from Anna to Dann

Seriously?

Email from Dann to Anna

No, completely unseriously I'm afraid – but I thought I'd get you back for testing my English with words like 'homogenous'!

Anyway, Grace told me you are a milliner? Is that even a proper job? 😜

Dann

Email from Anna to Dann

Dann

Touché!

Yes, millinery is a proper job, I will have you know, and anyway, someone has to do it otherwise we would have a world without gorgeous hats.

At school, I was just terrible at maths and abysmal at science but pretty good at art and English, and I was always a 'crafty' child. First and foremost, I wanted to be a writer. At one time or another, I was either in love with all the First World War poets or imagined myself as a tragic Pre-Raphaelite heroine and wrote terrible turgid prose.

Luckily, I was also dabbling with arts and crafts, sewing and needlecraft at the same time, and it soon became clear to everyone that, while I was never going to be the next Dante Gabriel Rossetti, there pretty much wasn't anything I couldn't make with fabric.

I certainly had the best dressed dolls and teddy bears when I was little. Our poor cat Cheddar got the Peel fashion makeover on more than one occasion. He was not best pleased, I can tell you, wearing his floral waistcoat I made from some old curtains!

My main love, though, was always design. I had a fanciful idea that I might like to be a fabric designer for Liberty but, as you can imagine, my careers advice teacher, Miss Hathaway, said that was quite specialist and she doubted there were many openings in that specific field. So she said, 'With your needlecraft skills and design flare, how about making hats instead?' She had just read up on a course being offered at a newly opened college in Kensington and thought it would be ideal for me.

So that is how it all began – a throwaway comment from a teacher who I suspect wished I was more interested in going to secretarial college or into catering.

Luckily, I discovered I did have a real flair for design and I also loved the technical side of hat-making. After college, I worked as a junior designer for a small artisan hat maker that had opened in Fulham High Road, and the rest is history. I took the plunge seven years ago to open my own design studio, and now have six staff and a pretty healthy business. It's amazing how much fabulously wealthy or famous women will pay for a bespoke hat that they can be confident they will never see on the head of any other fabulously wealthy or famous woman.

So, your turn, what's the story of Dann Huismann? Solider to teacher, the Netherlands to Africa. I'm intrigued – that is some career change!

Regards

Anna

Email from Dann to Anna

Anna

Well, it is nice to now be able to say 'I know a milliner', and I hope you weren't offended about the job comment – I think my English is fluent but I suspect sometimes the nuances of language let me down even now.

Grace showed me some sketches of your hat designs. I was very impressed. She said you are very talented, and I have to agree.

My career path does sound a bit drastic when you say it like that but is much more prosaic (I think that is the right word in English?) and not very exciting.

When I left school, I wasn't sure what to do. I was pretty good at languages, not bad at science, and really liked nature and travel, so ended up studying geography at university in Utrecht, which I hated – university not Utrecht, which is lovely.

After getting my degree, I had absolutely no idea what I wanted to do. The thought of teaching was definitely not on my radar then. I was still young and, frankly, a bit obnoxious. I had found study easy but tedious and had no clear plan of what I wanted to do apart from see the world. I think my parents were a bit alarmed that I was going to just drift aimlessly and waste my potential. It was actually nice they thought I had potential – I couldn't see it back then.

Before he retired from flying long-haul with KLM, my dad Jacob had been a pilot in the Royal Netherlands Air Force, and my mother Femke had been an army medic, so they were both great believers in the benefits of the military on wayward minds like mine.

I clearly remember my dad sitting me down and saying, 'Dann, you are a bright boy but your mother and I are worried you will waste your talent and you need some discipline.' He knew one of the training officers at the Royal Military Academy in Breda, and I am sure pulled a few strings to get me enrolled onto the next available officer training course.

Well, if I hated the regulation of university, I was in for a shock. Military life for new recruits is tough, particularly for an unruly youngster like me, but it wasn't long before they began to polish off some of my rougher edges and I actually started to relish the challenge and the structure. I was a good runner, a half-decent boxer and swimmer, and generally pretty fit back then, so excelled at physical training and was told I had good potential as a leader too, if only they could harness my ill-discipline.

So, I worked hard and was able to rise up through the officer ranks to Captain and fulfil my wish to see the world at the same time, although some of it I would rather forget. I managed two tours of Afghanistan before I got slightly broken on my last deployment. Thankfully it was nothing the doctors at the military hospital couldn't patch up, and I finally left army life behind me to see how I could use the skills I'd learned to be a productive Dutch civilian.

Sorry, just noticed the time. Got to go. I had completely forgotten it's football practice this afternoon and the kids will never forgive me if I am late, especially as I am always telling them about the importance of punctuality!

Part 2 – how I became a Geography teacher in Africa – to follow.

Best

Dann

Email from Anna to Izzy

Hey sis

I'm really enjoying this sponsorship experience. Henry is absolutely delightful and we have been sharing lots of letters about his family. I've also been writing to Grace Nkomo, who owns Baobab Tree Lodge and founded the school. She's a fascinating woman and has been telling me about Zambia and her life there. I'd forgotten how nice it is to write a proper letter to interesting people.

Love Anna

p.s. Oh, and BTW, I have also acquired a new 'pen-pal', see emails from Dann Huismann attached.

Email from Izzy to Anna

Hmm… disciplined, athletic, clever, decent. I like the sound of him!

Love Izzy x

✤

Email from Dann to Anna

Hi Anna

Football practice went on a bit longer than planned yesterday, so sorry I didn't email you back last night to wrap up the condensed history of Dann Huismann. Those kids could just keep running and running all evening, and wouldn't let me blow the final whistle until it was so dark we could hardly see the ball. I was glad when they called it a day. My slightly damaged leg means I can't run as far or for as long as I used to.

Part 2 of my story is pretty straightforward. After leaving the Forces, I went back to school to take my post-graduate certificate in education. I saw the post of Geography Teacher at Mwabonwa advertised and came here just over five years ago. The rest, as they say, is history.

That is the story of my life up to this point. I told you it wasn't very exciting.

I'd like to hear more about your family if you would like to tell me. I am an only child so having siblings and nieces and nephews is not something I have been lucky enough to experience.

Best

Dann

Email from Anna to Dann

Hi Dann

Yes, it's nice having an extended family although I sometimes think being an only child would be better – brothers and sisters can be really maddening sometimes.

I am the baby of the family, my brother Robbie is in the middle and my sister Izzy is the eldest, and by far the wisest. She and her lovely husband Tom, who is also a police officer, have three children who I call the BFG.

Anna

Email from Dann to Anna

Hi

Just showing I paid attention in English history class, are your Peels any relation to Sir Robert?

Dann

p.s. No idea what you mean by BFG?

Email from Anna to Dann

Hi Dann

Sadly no relation. My mum did do some genealogy once in the hope that she would find we had some sort of shared DNA that would explain why most of the family have gone into law enforcement, but there was no evidence we ever swam in the same exalted circles. It did mean though that they have all, at one time or another, been nicknamed Bobby by their colleagues!

Being surrounded by a family of police officers is a bit strange I suppose, but just what I'm used to. I always feel safe around them – I suppose that is the same with military families like yours too?

Back in the day, my mum and dad were both detectives in Major Crimes but have been retired for a while and now spend their gold-plated pensions cruising the world. Looking at my planner, I think they are currently somewhere around the New Zealand fjords!

Robbie is a Constable in Roads Policing up country. He isn't overly ambitious but loves driving fast cars. Izzy is a sergeant and has recently become the new Staff Officer to the Chief Constable.

As you can imagine, Christmas in our house was always interesting. I pity the poor neighbours who came round for sherry and mince pies and were regaled with not-very-festive anecdotes of grisly murders after my mum and dad had got a bit tipsy on pre-breakfast bubbles (only at Christmas, I hasten to add!). And have you ever seen four – five, after Tom arrived – competitive police officers playing Cluedo? I always thought it should be televised in a prime slot after the Queen's Speech.

So, as you can see, I am definitely the odd duck of the family, a celebrity hat-maker in a sea of gnarly coppers. No wonder my mum jokes that she thinks the hospital swapped me with her real baby at birth. Well, I'm pretty sure she's only joking! Seriously, they are all proud of me. Every time she goes to the hairdresser, my mum finds a copy of the latest style magazine or celebrity glossy lying around and flicks through it until she sees one of my hats, and then makes a point of showing everyone else in the salon, especially if it is on the head of a member of the royal family. Needless to say, she's a committed Royalist.

Oh sorry, yes, the BFG is a reference to Roald Dahl, just my little joke. The Peel family do have a long history of using quirky anagrams and initials all over the place! It is what I affectionately call my nieces and nephew. Belle is eleven and Izzy says they should have christened her Minnie-Anna as she is just like me. She loves to read and write, draw and make things. My nephew Freddie is nine and much more like Robbie was when he was that age, into all sorts of sports. Georgia is seven and a real little princess, although Izzy and

Tom think she will be the most academic when she is older. She already loves puzzles and maths so obviously takes after Tom, who is a bit of whizz with numbers too.

I don't see my brother as often as I would like, but Izzy and I are very close. There isn't anything in the world I wouldn't tell her.

Anna

Email from Dann to Anna

Anna

It must be nice to have someone you can share all your deepest, most personal secrets with. I envy you.

Dann

Email from Anna to Dann

Dann

Yes, I think we have a special bond. I love that she is so wise but she can also be cynical and a bit blunt – sometimes too blunt. If she thinks it, she says it, which can sometimes get her into hot water but, despite that, I always rely on her sound judgement. She's very good at reading people; I think that goes with her job.

And one thing I know is that she really doesn't understand the world I live in, but then neither do I when I think about it too deeply. I once invited her to a fashion week opening party being thrown by one of my acquaintances in Soho, which was very glamorous and packed with well-known faces. She said she enjoyed it but afterwards, she said, 'Anna, if you died tomorrow, none of those people would come to your funeral.' I told you she was blunt!

Actually, she is right. I can probably count the very good friends I have made in London on one hand. In my experience, love of celebrity means you keep friends only as long as they are useful to you.

Anna

Email from Dann to Anna

What about the ex-Mr Peel, is he a police officer too?

Email from Anna to Dann

No, he's a city trader in Canary Wharf. Definitely ex though, and thankfully not Mr Peel (he is a Tanner). I decided not to take his surname because my business was already well established when we got married, which was actually a blessing in the end. It meant I didn't have to change much when he upped sticks and left me, and anyway, my littlest niece Georgia thought it was hilarious that I could have been Anna Tanner.

I try to remember what he was like when we first met. Certainly very attractive and nice, I think, although Izzy calls him 'obvious' and not in a complimentary way. Let's just say, he found moving in the circles that developed around me because of my work much easier than I ever did and it didn't take him long to develop a rather unedifying taste for expensive trinkets and influential people.

He also had a somewhat cruel side. He was never physical,

thank God, but I vividly remember him once saying, 'Anna, for all your talent you have 'imposter syndrome' written all over you. If you can't fit into this lifestyle, make way for those of us who can.'

Anna

He sounds like a jerk.

Dann

I couldn't disagree, but he was *my* jerk – at least I thought he was – and I did love him once.

It still hurts a bit, although now I think it's bruised pride more than anything. To add insult to injury, he eventually left me for a tall, blonde coffee heiress with old-money connections and celebrity friends, not just celebrity 'clients' like I had. At the end of the day, Matt wanted to be *in* the in-crowd, not just happy watching on from the sidelines like me.

Anyway, enough of my pointless ranting, I've heard reliving stressful things can be very bad for the complexion and I don't have time for a break-out at the moment.

Anyway, what about you? Grace told me you had a wife and child but they died.

Anna

November

Hi Dann

I haven't heard from you for a couple of weeks, is all okay? Was it my crass and insensitive question about your wife and child? I am so, so sorry. As soon as I pressed send I realised I'd overstepped the mark.

Anna

Email from Dann to Anna

Sorry, I've been busy at school and with the Arts Centre, but if it's okay, I would just rather not talk about my family. Perhaps one for another day.

Dann

Dann

Truly, I didn't mean to pry. Grace was just telling me about losing her daughter Elisabeth and she mentioned you had also suffered a similar bereavement. I don't think she meant to break a confidence, so please don't be cross with her.

Anna

Anna

No need to apologise, and I'm not angry with Grace. Perhaps she thought it would make you take pity on me, but please don't. I struggle to wear the mantle of tragic figure very comfortably.

I think Grace is just frustrated by her lack of success so is upping her game – is that how you say it?

Perhaps one day I will tell you more about the time she coerced me into taking a pretty Korean guest out onto the river to look at the birds, even though Piet was available, and she forbade me to come back for the whole morning. I am not fluent by any means, but I can make myself understood in Korean (long story), and I spent the entire trip hearing about how she was only in Zambia to see the Falls and sit in the Devil's Pool so she could get endless selfies to make her friends jealous on her various social media platforms and her YouTube hair and make-up channel. She had absolutely no interest in the wildlife whatsoever and, thankfully, she also had zero interest in me, but I can tell you it was a very long four hours.

Or the disastrous blind date Grace set me up on with the daughter of her church pastor, the very nice and marvellously named Jeremiah Johnson-Johnson. Let's just say it didn't end well and involved food poisoning, a sprained ankle and the unexpected appearance of an enormous wolf spider.

All I know is that, six years on, it is no easier.

This pen-pal thing is harder than I thought it was going to be. Much easier when you are ten and can just talk about football and cars and pop music.

Dann

Email from Anna to Dann

Dann

Let's pretend to be ten then.

1. Football - Robbie once had a trial for a minor league club near where we grew up so I spent a lot of wet Saturday afternoons cheering on from the touchline. When I first came to London, I used to go to Chelsea to watch them play as I had a crush on a boy from college called James who was an avid fan so – probably out of character for a girly milliner – I know a surprising amount about football. Who do you support?
2. Cars – I don't drive now I live in London, but my first car was a Mini Clubman with psychedelic orange paintwork and a temperamental choke. My fantasy car would be a Mercedes-Benz convertible from the 1970s in powder blue – it is so chic.

3. Pop Music – I love anything soulful or with a jazz vibe (and definitely *not* gangster rap!) and I have even been known to channel my inner Whitney at karaoke, but very, very badly.

Hope that helps us reset to less personal subjects, but always happy to be here if you want to talk.

Write soon.

Anna

Email from Dann to Anna

1. 'Ga Ajax' all the way. I hope James appreciated you understanding the offside rule. When you are a young boy who likes football, that is a very alluring quality in a young girl.
2. First car – beaten-up Honda Accord
Current car – the school pick-up!
Ideal car – the school pick-up!
3. I don't know what gangster rap is, but it doesn't sound very healthy. I would say I have an eclectic mix of musical tastes. I like a bit of opera every now and then, but definitely no karaoke. I can count my talents on one hand and singing is not one of them. About a hundred years ago I played piano too, but I haven't touched a keyboard for years so imagine I would be pretty rusty now.

Dann

p.s. Thank you.

Dear Anna

I almost forgot, I promised to write and tell you more about our wonderful baobab tree.

When we arrived here, the ground was covered in a knotted tangle of native scrub plants, trees and grasses, much of which we needed to clear to rebuild the Lodge. Joseph was marvellous with native plants, so knew exactly which ones to keep and cultivate, and which to dig up.

However, as the bank rises away from the Zambezi, up the hill, and turns slightly upriver from the property, there was a flattish patch of sandy ground and, right in the middle of it, dominating the surrounding area, was an old baobab tree that we estimated was at least fifty feet tall.

Now, the native baobab is a very special tree in Africa. Legend has it that the gods along the Zambezi thought the tree stood too straight and proud so, to teach it a lesson for its arrogance and conceit, they uprooted it and threw it back into the ground upside down. I've attached a photo of our tree – you can definitely see why it is sometimes called the upside down tree!

We don't know how old our tree is. It could be six hundred years old. There is one on the Zimbabwe side of the Falls that is believed to be over a thousand years old, and I think ours is just as impressive. We say the baobab tree is resourceful like the people of Africa, and I once heard it called 'probably the most useful tree of all', which I could not disagree with.

Not only can it store water in its branches and trunk, which helped sustain ancient man during the dry season, but it can be used as shelter – you will see ours is hollow and easily large enough for a man to stand in – and some of the locals says it is where pregnant women used to go to give birth. You can eat the leaves, roots, fruit and seeds, it has many medicinal uses, and the fibrous bark makes excellent cloth.

It seemed only fitting to name our lodge after the tree, as resourcefulness is something we truly valued. Today, it is certainly one of the many natural wonders along our part of the Zambezi that our guests like to photograph!

With all best wishes

Grace

✻

Email from Anna to Izzy

Izzy

Am I a bad person?

Anna x

Email from Izzy to Anna

Hmm… that sounds like a leading question.

On balance, I would say not, but depends on what you've done.

OMG, you haven't done Matt in, have you? I'm not sure it would do my career prospects any good being the sister of a murderess! 😜

Izzy x

Email from Anna to Izzy

No of course not – however tempting.

I googled Dann Huismann's wife. Grace told me her name was Anika and now I feel like I've gone behind his back when I know he didn't want to share any information about her.

Anna x

Email from Izzy to Anna

Phew! Is that all?

Hardly makes you Public Enemy No. 1. Who hasn't Googled an ex or a new mate? I've told Belle that when she starts dating – which, by the way, won't be before she's thirty if me and her dad have anything to do with it – it's the first thing I'm going to do with any potential suitor. Either that or take a sneaky look on the police national computer, but don't tell Tom. It's a definite no-no to look for personal reasons and it would be embarrassing if I ended up on the opposite side of the desk from him under investigation lol!

Anyway, can't believe you didn't Google 'Miss Stick' when you first found out about her and Matt (know your enemy etc). I know I did! I didn't tell you because, sadly, she is just as lovely as you suspected.

Anyway, more importantly, what did you find out?

Izzy xx

Email from Anna to Izzy

Nothing much.

There was just one report from a local newspaper but

it was in Dutch (obviously). There was a picture of a really smashed-up car but no other details I could make out, so looks like they died in a car accident.

☹

p.s. Dann Huismann is definitely not my 'new mate', he is just someone I write to.

*

Email from Grace to Anna

Dear Anna

I have been looking back through my photo albums at when we first came to the Lodge. Don't you think it is a shame that young people now just seem to take photographs on their phones and never print them and put them in an album? There is nothing nicer than sitting down and holding something so tangible in your hands, and it has given me great pleasure to travel back in time and to see Samuel and I at the very start. I had forgotten how slim and pretty I was back then!

I think I've already mentioned this, but when we first arrived, it was obvious the property just wasn't habitable, let alone in any state to receive paying visitors. The Lodge buildings were run down and needed a lot of work to even make them safe for us, let alone turn it into the beautiful property it is today. Luckily, Samuel had a business brain as well as a mathematical one, I was the 'creative director' and Joseph was in charge of landscaping, planting and wildlife so, between us, we had most of the skills we needed.

The main lodge house was substantial in size and had obviously once been very grand, but was in poor repair with peeling boards, a sagging wooden porch and broken windows. Worse still, the roof had collapsed at one end of what we now call the east wing (doesn't that make it sound grand? It really isn't!) and several Zambian wet seasons had ruined the walls and floors beyond repair.

There were signs that the house had, at one time, also had a pretty cultivated garden but, having been left for many years, the native bush had reclaimed it, even though we thought we could see some very old and gnarled rosebushes amongst the grasses and acacia trees. There was also a small greenhouse and summer house, both of which were derelict, and a broken jetty leading into the river.

Thankfully, when Samuel's grandparents passed away, they left him their house – the one he had spent his childhood holidays in over the border. He was the only son of an only son, so it was only natural that the property would come to him. It was very small and, in truth, a bit shabby, but perfectly serviceable for our needs. Most importantly, it was only twenty miles from the Lodge so we could travel back and forth across the border every day.

And so the work began and, believe me, it was hard, back-breaking work.

We weren't short of labour, which was a good thing. As now, finding work was often hard for the local men, and many of them would sit at one or two shady spots in Livingstone each morning at dawn before the heat of the day drove them away, waiting for a local landowner or construction boss to seek them out to do a day's paid work. We had an old, battered flatbed truck so, on the way to the Lodge each day, we picked up Joseph from his home and then as many men as we needed for the day's work. Depending on what we needed to do that day, sometimes there were three or four, sometimes up to ten.

We soon realised that if we waited until the Lodge was completely renovated and the new holiday cottages finished, we would run out of money. We did have some outbuildings that we were going to convert but many of the cottages we have now had to be built new, so we needed to think of a way of promoting ourselves as a viable business to help pay the bills as soon as we could.

And that is where Musanga Island come to the rescue. Do you remember I wrote that we also bought a small island at the same time as the mainland property, which we named after the umbrella tress dotted all about? In fact, while we were rebuilding the Lodge, it was Musanga Island that we used as our first wilderness venture. We were accidental champions and early adopters of eco-tourism before it became the popular thing to do, although I have to admit that back then it was largely driven by a lack of any basic amenities, like hot water or electricity, rather than by any conscious ethical principles.

It is about three miles upstream from the Lodge and measures about a quarter of a mile from end to end. Apart from the umbrella trees, which gave some lovely dappled shade, the native bush was sparse and easily cut back, and there were also two small sandy beach areas on the side of the island facing across the water to Zimbabwe on the opposite bank, which at that point is only about three hundred feet or so.

One of the beaches was ideal to land a small flat-bottomed boat, with the addition of some chicken wire to protect our boat – and us – from the crocodiles that sometimes hide in the reeds at the water's edge. The other beach was more secure as it had the benefit of a fairly high bank surrounding it, so we left that as it was for any passing wildlife that wanted to wander up and rest. Today, we actually have a semi-resident hippo that the children at Mwabonwa have named Brian. Brian calls this beach his home and can be seen sunbathing there most mornings. He is definitely what our visitors call a 'crowd pleaser' and must be one of the most photographed hippos in Zambia!

We later acquired a boat, complete with outboard motor, from a cousin of Joseph's who had decided to give up fishing on the Zambezi and move upcountry to find more lucrative work in the mines. As with most things we had back then, it was perfectly functional, if a little tired, but looked quite stylish with a new coat of yellow paint and lacquer, some home-made cushions and a canopy that Samuel fashioned out of canvas. We called her Lucy and, although she is no longer safe to take on the water – the Zambezi is a very dangerous river – we keep her freshly painted and tied up at the old jetty to remind us of the journey we have been on.

I will tell you more about our early days on the island when I next write. We certainly had some very interesting experiences, particularly with wildlife!

Love

Grace

Letter from Henry to Anna

Dear Miss Anna

I am very sad today so Daddy said I should write to you, as that always makes me feel a bit better.

Mr Huismann was letting me help him count the blocks he needs to make the walls and stack them behind the Arts Centre when he found an injured baby vervet monkey in the scrub bush. It looked like it had been caught in one of the home-made snares that some of the men put around the area to catch wild pigs. It had lost its tail and was just lying lifeless on the ground. Mr Huismann thought it was dead but it grasped his finger when he touched it, so he picked it up and we brought it back to his house.

Esther gave him a cardboard box that her printer paper came in, which Mr Huismann lined with an old jumper. When he dripped some water into the baby monkey's mouth, its eyes flickered open for a moment.

Mr Huismann told me it would still probably die, as it was too young to be without its mother and that it wouldn't be able to return to the trees without a tail. He looked very serious but he didn't say it unkindly, I think he was just trying to be honest with me.

I said I knew he was going to make it better and that when he did, I was going to call the monkey Chutu and have it as a pet. Mr Huismann said that it wouldn't be fair to keep it as a pet as vervet are social animals that live in big family groups, and that I shouldn't give it a name. I said, 'Please, please make him better Mr Huismann.' Mr Huismann sighed and looked stern again but he said he would see what he could do.

That was on Wednesday and I've visited Chutu every day after school. It is Saturday today and there was a knock on the door just as the light was creeping in through the window of my room and I was just thinking about getting up early to do my chores so I could go and play football with Boston.

My daddy opened the door and Mr Huismann was there with the little box in his hands. He looked tired and sad, and he didn't need to say anything as I knew Chutu had died. Daddy let Mr Huismann sit in his special armchair and I was allowed to stroke Chutu's fur for a while. He looked very peaceful. I didn't want Mr Huismann to see me cry so I bit my lip. My mother went and got a piece of amasuku fruit and a bunch of wild herbs from the garden, which she let me place in the box.

Mr Huismann said that if I liked, we could bury Chutu near where we had found him so he would be close to his mother in the trees. I said I would like that very much.

Later on, we went and dug a hole in the scrub bush behind the Arts Centre. Mr Huismann placed the box in the ground and gently covered it with dirt. He said 'Dear Lord, we commit the soul of this baby monkey to your care. Please let him grow his tail back so he can once more play among the highest celestial branches with his ancestors.'

I then did feel a big fat, hot tear rolling down my cheek and it landed in the sandy dirt on top of the little grave. I don't think Mr Huismann saw but he did put his hand on my shoulder, which felt nice, and we stood for a moment in silence. As it was Saturday and there was no school, he then asked me if I wanted him to teach me how to mix mortar, so that's what we did.

When I came back later, someone had made a small cross out of two rough pieces of pallet wood bound together with garden twine. The cross had CHUTU written on it and the date. I know that wasn't Mr Huismann as he told me not to name the baby monkey, so perhaps it was Esther?

I found a fallen branch of a thorn tree on the ground behind our house so I put that on top of the grave too in case Chutu's spirit needed a reminder about how to get to the treetops.

I haven't chosen a word of the day today because I am still sad, but Daddy was right, I do feel better for writing to you.

Love

Henry

Email from Anna to Dann

Dear Dann

I've had a letter from Henry telling me about the baby monkey. Don't think I'm being over-sentimental but I have literally just stopped crying. He said you did everything you could to keep it alive and also what you said at the graveside, which was beautiful and very moving. Wasn't it lovely of Esther to put up a marker too.

Anna

Email from Dann to Femke Huismann

Hoi Mama

Hoe gaat het met je? Is papa's rug beter?

Mama, ik wilde je gewoon laten weten da ik iemand heb ontmoet. Nou, ik heb haar niet precies ontmoet. Ik weet nog niet zeker of het ergens heen gaat, misschien nergens, maar ik zal je laten weten wanneer ik dat doe.

Liefs jullie beiden.

Dann xx

Email from Dann to Anna

Hi Anna

Of course I don't think you're being over-sentimental. I felt sad too, although I put that down to being pretty tired after staying up for three nights trying to keep it alive.

I suppose I just didn't want to let Henry down, as he seems to think I am some sort of miracle worker. I did everything I could but no amount of midnight feeds was going to help, I'm afraid. I am glad he liked what I said, though. I'm not religious but it felt appropriate somehow.

In the end, it was just its time to go, and I think Henry understands that now. People are generally less sentimental about death here.

Oh, and please don't tell Henry, but I put up the grave marker. I felt I was a bit harsh when I told him not to name the monkey, and I thought it might give him some comfort.

Dann xx

Email from Dann to Anna

Just noticed the 'xx' on my email – totally inappropriate, sorry! I was emailing my mother at the same time.

Email from Anna to Izzy

Izzy, read this. I haven't been able to stop crying for the last ten minutes.

A xx

Email from Izzy to Anna

OMG – that is literally the saddest thing. 😞

Anyway, more importantly, Mr Huismann? What did I say before – disciplined, athletic, clever and decent? I think you can now add dishy, strong, brave, educated but practical, nurturer of small children and carer for dying animals. If Matt was the Ratt, is Dann the Mann??

Izzy

Email from Anna to Izzy

Have you been drinking?

Email from Izzy to Anna

Anna

Very funny, you know I never touch a drop before noon and certainly not when I'm in uniform!

You have to agree that, on the surface, Dann does seem to be ticking some 'ideal-man-aka-Mr-Darcy' type boxes. Granted, he could actually be a serial killer or perhaps he has a fetish for stilettos or model trains or spends his spare time sitting in the dark playing online Dungeons & Dragons like some overgrown man-child. Worse still, perhaps he is like Matt (no offence, I know you married him!).

Or, perhaps, he is actually, literally perfect?

Izzy

Email from Anna to Izzy

None taken ref. Matt.

Just because Dann cares for small children and animals, has a brain and can lay a breeze block does not necessarily make him Mr Right!!!! Oh, and if you hadn't noticed, he lives on the other side of the world.

Email from Izzy to Anna

Goodness, four exclamation marks from you and two Freudian kisses from him. Interesting! 😊

December

Email from Grace to Anna

Dearest Anna

Merry Christmas from Zambia.

Although I don't always feel it, when I look in the mirror each morning I know I am old. And yet, sometimes, something happens that makes me realise that every day there are new surprises and possibilities, even if you have more years behind you than in front of you.

So, I had to write and tell you that I had the strangest but most joyous experience yesterday. Dann popped over to my apartments because he wanted to check the Lodge rota over Christmas. He is so very thoughtful. The school is closed, of course, and he doesn't need to work but he always offers to help out here so that other members of staff can have time off with their families. He says, 'Grace, I may not be the best administrator in the world, but I can answer the phone and help with guest queries in Esther's absence, if that's useful.'

I was busying myself getting my planner out when he

suddenly sat down at Samuel's piano. Samuel wasn't a very good pianist but he did like to play occasionally, mostly quite simple tunes. Dann started to pick out one or two random notes and then, to my utter amazement, he started to play. I recognised it instantly as Mozart's Minuet in F as it was one of Samuel's favourites. I think you have an expression about your chin hitting the floor – well, thankfully I know that is figurative not literal, although that is exactly what I felt.

I was almost moved to tears, it is such a beautiful piece. I said, 'Dann, you've been here for five years and I never knew you could play the piano.' He said he hadn't touched a keyboard since he left the Netherlands but he just saw Samuel's piano looking quiet and a bit unloved and thought he would try to remember how to play. He obviously could remember and it was absolutely lovely to hear the piano being used properly for the first time. I said he could come over and use it whenever the mood took him so I do hope he will. It was utterly magical to hear the house filled with music again after such a long time.

Wishing you and your family a most wonderful holiday.

Love

Grace x

Email from Anna to Dann

Dear Dann

Vrolijk Kerstfeest!

I hope that's right, I googled it!

Just wanted to drop you a short email to wish you a happy Christmas, although Grace has already told me you will probably be working for most of it. I am just finishing my packing as I'm going to stay with my sister and her family in Devon for a few days. It's lovely to be around small children at Christmas but I'm not that used to the heat, chaos and noise – children can really ratchet up the decibels when they are excited! I plan to be back in my wonderfully serene flat the day after Boxing Day.

I hope you manage to get some time off and that you are able to speak with your mother and father. I am sure they miss you, particularly at this time of year.

Wishing you a wonderful Christmas and a peaceful new year.

Love Anna

p.s. Grace told me about you playing Samuel's piano – she was absolutely delighted but totally surprised that she didn't even know you could play. I won't take any credit but perhaps mentioning it to me prompted you to play again after so many years? If so, I'm very pleased, and if you have a real gift like that, you must never lose it.

Email from Mr Munyama to Anna

Dear Miss Peel

Happy Christmas from Mwabonwa School.

I wanted to write on behalf of the whole school, particularly Mr Nkoso, our librarian, and the geography department, for your very kind gift. We have not had such a magnificent atlas in our possession before, and I am not sure I have ever seen one so large or so detailed. We will keep it in pride of place on the main library table and the children will be able to come over and look at it whenever they would like to – under strict supervision, of course.

Kind regards and best wishes

Mr Munyama, Head Teacher

Letter and parcel from Anna to Henry

Dear Henry

I just wanted to write to say I hope you and your family have a lovely Christmas. I promise your daddy I am not spoiling you, so hope he will be happy for you to have this present to open on the day. It is something you can share with your friend Boston. I hope you like it.

I will write again in the new year.

Love

Anna x

Email from Dann to Anna

Dear Anna

Merry Christmas too!

I hope you have a lovely time in Devon, it sounds chaotic but wonderful in equal measure.

Thanks for asking about my mother and father. We normally have a video call on Christmas morning. My mother always says, 'Dann, we miss you,' shortly followed by my dad saying, 'Dann, please shave off your beard'!

I'm a bit old for presents but they do usually send me a

food parcel to celebrate – stuff you can't get here like Kerststol and Dutch chocolate, so I am sure I will find some free time to over-indulge like everyone else.

By the way, thank you from me for the new school atlas. It was very thoughtful of you.

And thank you for asking about the piano. Not sure why I started to play it, it looked a bit forlorn just sitting in the corner and I can't remember the last time I actually heard music coming from it… perhaps three years ago. Samuel, by his own admission, was enthusiastic but not very technically proficient, and I have to admit my fingers did feel rusty to start with. I'm sure there were one or two wrong notes but Grace was too polite to mention them. I was pleasantly surprised at how much I could remember, though. Perhaps it is like that English saying about riding a bike?

Enjoy your Christmas and I look forward to catching up with you in the new year.

Dann x

p.s. I've dropped a small Christmas gift in the post to you, although knowing the Zambian postal service, you may not get it until Easter! I hope, when it does eventually arrive in England, you like it.

Email from Anna to Izzy

Hey

Just a quick one, I'll see you on the 22nd. I'll be juggling my bag and quite a few presents, so can you or Tom pick me up from St David's? I'll be on the 10:20 train from Paddington so, barring any delays, getting in about 12:30-ish? I'll text you when I get to the other side of Tiverton Parkway.

Love

Anna x

Email from Izzy to Anna

Hi sis

I'm off that day so no worries. I'll be waiting outside. We can't wait to see you – the BFG are extremely excited so I hope you've packed your earplugs!!

Love

Izzy x

January

Happy New Year Miss Anna

Henry's word of the day: GENEALOGY
Thank you so much for the football. I wondered what it was as the box was so large but light. I have already been out every morning since Christmas playing with Boston. We drew a goal on the side of the old garage wall at the school with some chalk and have been taking it in turns to be Mweene, the goalkeeper, and Mayuka, the striker.

We are now back at school after the holidays and we have been asked in our Social Responsibility and Community class to write an essay about our family history, starting with our mothers and fathers. Miss Banda says looking at the lineage of our ancestry is sometimes called genealogy, and I thought you would be interested to know more about us too.

My daddy was born and raised in Kitwe in the north of Zambia, in the Copperbelt Province. I have never been but Daddy says it is the second largest city in Zambia and is very industrial. The soil of Zambia contains many riches, like cobalt and emeralds, but is most famous for its copper. Nearly every man and boy in Kitwe works in one of the many copper mines in the district, and my daddy's own daddy was a copper miner all his life. My daddy has vivid memories of seeing his father when he came home each evening, white from head to toe with the dust that would stick to his sweat. My daddy said it made him scared, as if his daddy was a ghost, but every evening his mother put the old tin bath out on their porch and would bathe his father clean as she sang to him. Although they were poor – my daddy says it is a great sadness that in such a rich country, many people have hard lives and never get any richer – he was lucky in that he was a bright child and studied hard at school. He always had a love of nature and plants and remembers spending hours with his grandmother, who had a tiny kitchen garden and who my daddy said knew everything about plants to use as medicines. If you had a toothache or an upset tummy, she would make teas and tinctures from her plants that worked better than anything you could buy in a shop. She also loved to cook and sing. When he was fifteen, Daddy was lucky enough to win a scholarship to the Red Cedar Horticultural School in Ndola. Perhaps that is why he says to me, 'Henry, the harder you work, the luckier you get.'

His parents were very proud of him as they didn't want him to become a miner. My daddy says it was hard to start with, as he didn't know anyone in Ndola, but a local pastor and his wife gave him lodgings, and he studied during the day and worked at the local food market in the evening to pay his way. He says working there and spending time with his grandmother are what gave him his love of cooking too.

My mother is originally from Mbala but moved to Livingstone when Grandad Arnold found work here. Daddy says Mbala is as far north in Zambia as you can go before you become a Tanzanian, and very close to Kalambo Falls, which are the second highest in all of Africa. Daddy says our Falls are not the tallest in Africa but are one of the widest in the world and he thinks they are even more spectacular than Kalambo, and he has seen them both. I have never seen our waterfall but I think Mr Huismann is planning a geography field trip for us to Mosi-oa-Tunya one day soon.

Mother met Daddy when he started to work at the Lodge as she was already working here as a maid. Although she is twenty years younger than him, she says my daddy was an advantageous match for her. Many people say my mother is very beautiful and I agree, although Daddy sometimes calls her mischievous. I have also heard Daddy call my mother wilful and stubborn, but he is never cruel to her and they spend a lot of time hugging.

My mother sometimes pats his huge tummy and says, 'You are even starting to look like one of your beloved watermelons, old man,' but I know she loves him very much.

Love

Henry x

Email from Anna to Dann

Dear Dann

Happy new year.

I am just waiting at St Pancras station to catch an early train to Paris for a meeting with a new client, but couldn't leave without sending you an email to say thank you so much for my Christmas present. It is the most beautiful stone I have ever seen. It is currently in my pocket so I can take a little piece of Zambia with me wherever I go.

I'd love to know what it is and where you found it.

Anna

Email from Dann to Anna

Hi Anna

Gelukkig nieuwjaar!

I'm so glad you like it. I picked it up the last time I was down in Victoria Falls gorge in the dry season. It's a full day's hike and not for the faint-hearted but a must-do for any serious geologist. The stone was quite dull when I found it but it polished up nicely. I'm usually more knowledgeable about rocks if they are brown or grey but, given its shade of pink, I think it is probably a rose quartz (but don't quote me on that!).

Anyway, I'm glad you like it.

Regards

Dann

Email from Grace to Anna

Dear Anna

Happy new year from Zambia.

How are you in London? I hope you are well and have had an enjoyable Christmas. We had a lovely time here. Our guests love all the festivities and I get George and Thomas to put up as many fairy lights as possible, which makes the whole property sparkle in the dark.

I think it is your winter season, so is it cold there? We don't have the same seasons like you do there, we just have wet and dry. I have never been to England but Samuel used to like old black and white films, I think from Ealing Studios. Is it always that foggy in London, and does it snow as much as I see on all the old Christmas films?

It is very hot here at the moment. We have air conditioning in the guest accommodation, of course, but not in the offices. They are all open-sided so the breeze is lovely but it is still very warm.

I have been working at the computer in the office this morning. Esther is so busy and some invoices needed checking so I offered to help. I am not convinced she thought I would be able to do it but I shooed her away, although I have to confess I had forgot how reconciling numbers starts to blur after a while.

So I thought I would take a short break and write to you instead. Esther has gone on her rounds so she won't know she was absolutely right after all.

I found a photo yesterday of Samuel, Joseph and our very first paying guests, Lily and Gregor. I forget their surname but I think they were from Durban. They are standing next to our little tented camp on Musanga Island and I realised I hadn't told you about our first experiences there.

Renovation at the Lodge was in full swing but as I think I said, it was soon obvious it was going to take us longer than we had anticipated, and we were rapidly running out of money. We were brainstorming ideas one night after dinner and Joseph said, 'We have the island. Is there a market for wilderness camping? If so, we might just need some tents!'

It sounds so simple now but back then, we had no idea if anyone would even want to come from the comfort of their own homes to stay in a tent without any amenities on an island in the middle of the Zambezi.

I think I mentioned that Samuel was an only child, but he had a first cousin once removed called Charlotte who worked as a travel agent in Cape Town, and another, Jeffrey, who was in advertising in Harare. There was no internet back then of course, so Samuel phoned them both to pitch our idea. I am not sure Jeffrey was convinced but, despite his misgivings, he kindly offered to draft a basic design for our wilderness camp adventures. He did advise the word 'holiday' might not be appropriate! Charlotte agreed to circulate it to her colleagues across southern Africa. We were very fortunate to have their help, and perhaps that is serendipity.

We planned what we would need as the very basic. We thought tents, of course, but as a bare minimum, we would also need some way of cooking and keeping our guests warm at night, as well as drinking water and sanitation.

Joseph and Samuel took the flatbed truck into Livingstone to pay a visit to our very good Army and Navy Surplus store, somewhat inappropriately – I think – called 'The War Warehouse'. They returned with four used military tents as well as camouflage netting, nearly new sleeping bags, camp beds and four pairs of ex-navy binoculars, second-hand but robust and in good working order. They also went to Harvey's Happy Hardware and bought rope, buckets, chicken wire, shovels and cooking utensils.

They cleared the ground in the very centre of the island where the vegetation was quite light and built a large fire pit using rocks they found dotted around the river banks. They erected the tents near the fire and, at the eastern end of the island, constructed a very basic shower out of a bucket strung with rope from a tree, which they filled each morning from the river. I won't tell you too much about the toilet facilities, except to say that each tent had its own shovel and a patch of sandy soil surrounded by some privacy fencing at the opposite end of the island – a DIY latrine! I laugh now when I think about it. Even though our guests today enjoy the 'wilderness' experience, they rarely like to do it without hot water, fluffy towels and, above all, a flushing toilet!

And so 'Musanga Island Wilderness Adventures' was born.

We waited with bated breath, I think you would say, and it was only two weeks later that Charlotte said she had an enquiry from Lily and Gregor (thinking about it, they may have been from Port Elizabeth?) asking about our camp. They taught botany and environmental sciences respectively and wanted to see the Falls and our wildlife in as natural a setting as possible.

Well, we pulled out all the stops to make sure they had an amazing experience, which they did, and they gave Charlotte such a glowing review when they returned home that the bookings just started to flow in.

I hope one day, if you are ever able to come to Zambia, you will be able to experience the magic of Musanga for yourself. I can promise you you wouldn't be disappointed.

Love

Grace

Email from Izzy to Anna

Quickie – I told one of Belle's friend's mums about you being given a rose quartz for Christmas, I know she's into all that crystal stuff. She says whoever gave it to you must like you very much as it is known as the crystal of unconditional love and is used to foster loving relationships with others.

Do you think Dann knew that when he gave it to you or is that just a happy co-incidence?

Love

Izzy xx

Email from Anna to Izzy

He's a geologist, not a crystalologist (is that even a word)? I imagine where rocks are concerned, his interest stops at igneous, sedimentary or metamorphic (shows I did pay attention in geography class).

Anna xx

Letter from Henry to Anna

Dear Miss Anna

The best news ever! Mr Huismann has organised a trip to Mosi-oa-Tunya for our geography year. We will be going with Mr Huismann and Mr Tembo, our Deputy Head Teacher who also teaches history, as we are going to visit Livingstone Museum on the same day.

Mr Munyama is organising a minibus to collect us and we will be away from school all day, and then have to write an essay about what we have learned.

I will write again soon to tell you about our day.

Love

Henry x

�֍

Letter from Henry to Anna

Dear Miss Anna

Henry's words of the day: Awe-inspiring, Overwhelming, Breath-taking, Fearsome, Majestic, Humbling, Hypnotic
Today is Sunday and we went on our trip to Mosi-oa-Tunya on Friday. I would have written before now, but I was behind on my chores so yesterday I had to clean out the chickens, watch the twins while my mother went to the local village market to buy sugar, soya and vegetable oil, and then help my father repair the canes that hold up his okra plants. Some wild pigs had been through his vegetable patch and knocked them over. He was angry but also pleased that the sturdy posts and netting he put in last year meant they weren't able to eat all his vegetables. I got up extra early today to write, as I will have to get ready for church soon.

We set off in our minibus at about 10 o'clock. It is very wet here at the moment but hot. We got soaked just running from the school to the minibus so we were all steaming a bit by the time we got to the Falls, which are about twenty-five minutes' drive away. Mama Grace had very kindly let us borrow some of the heavy oiled raincoats that she keeps for when her guests visit the Falls in the rainy season, to help keep us dry.

We had to go through the checkpoint on the main road as we left the nature reserve, and I thought the guards there looked very scary with their military uniforms and big guns, but they just waved us through as they were too busy dealing with a large truck that was parked on the side of the road. Mr Tembo said it had Zimbabwean number plates so was being checked for poachers.

We drove through Livingstone, which was so bright and colourful with all the Friday market stalls. They seem to sell everything at the market, and there were lots of people looking at the poultry and vegetables, fabric, pots, pans, tyres, garden equipment, books, tools and more. There were a lot of young women with little babies strapped to their backs and huge earthen pots on their heads. They are not as beautiful as my mother, but Daddy says Zambian women have the strongest necks in the world.

When we got to the Falls, we parked near the main entrance. There is a separate market there, with some small shops and more covered stalls. Mr Tembo said the traders there mostly make and sell goods to tourists. I saw a man carving a piece of wood into the shape of an elephant. He was holding it between his bare feet and using a chisel that looked very sharp. I was worried he might slip and cut off his toe!

There was also a shop with a large rack outside covered in yards of brightly coloured chitenge fabric. One of the fabrics had a design of red, green and blue elephants, giraffes and crocodiles. I thought my mother would love it to make dresses for the twins, but it would be far too expensive.

My classmates and I were a bit scared to get out of the minibus as there was a big group of baboons milling about in the car park. One of them was almost as tall as I am and looked very fierce with its enormous teeth bared. Mr Tembo said, 'Do not worry, just ignore them. They are always here looking for food, they will do you no harm.' He was right that none of the traders or tourists seemed to be concerned, so we got out, put on our raincoats and walked quite fast to the main gate. Mr Huismann teased us that we all looked funny. The coats are huge and mine was almost touching the ground.

It is about a ten-minute walk to the first lookout and by the time we got there, the rain had turned from heavy to torrential and our hair, faces, legs and feet were all drenched through, even though the coats did keep the rain off our clothes. Mr Tembo had water dripping from his nose, and Mr Huismann's feet were squelching in his shoes.

I have never seen anything in my life like the Falls, and probably will never see anything like them again if I live to be one hundred! They are huge, nearly 6,000 feet from end to end, and it hurt my eyes to try to look at it all at once. The noise of the water was so loud that I could feel it vibrating in my chest, and we couldn't hear each other without shouting. I don't think we moved for a full ten minutes, we just stood and stared as if we were hypnotised.

There was also the most beautiful rainbow across the water. On the way home Mr Huismann said this is caused by the constant spray and Mr Tembo said some local people actually call the falls Seongo or Chongwe, which mean the 'Place of the Rainbow'.

After a while, we moved along the stone path, which

wends up and down, so that we could get different views. There was also a long rope bridge across one of the side gorges, which was great fun and a bit scary all at the same time. We laughed all the way across but I was glad when I got to the other side.

When we got to the last gorge lookout, Mr Huismann asked a pretty American tourist lady if she would take our photo, so he gave her his camera and we all posed with the Falls in the background. He says he will ask Esther to print a copy for each of us to have, but I asked for two so I can send one to you. I hope to have it by next time I write.

As we were walking down the path, we said hello to David Livingstone. There is a large bronze statue of him near the first lookout, just gazing out in wonder across the water. Mr Tembo said he was the first white man to see the Falls in 1855. I can't imagine what he thought when he came through the bush, or what he thought all that noise was.

I have to end now as Mother is calling me as I am not dressed yet, so I will write and tell you about the museum next time, and send my photo too, I hope.

I couldn't decide on one word of the day. I asked Mr Nkosi which was the best word to choose to describe Mosi-oa-Tunya and he said that in his humble opinion, one word could not do it justice. So he let me look at his big thesaurus but, as I couldn't decide on just one either, I have chosen seven (and two have hyphens!) which will always make me think of my very first visit.

Love Henry x

Email from Anna to Dann

Hello Dann

Hope all well at Mwabonwa. I hope you haven't been washed away. Henry tells me the rain has been relentless lately.

He has written to tell me about his trip to Victoria Falls, it sounds utterly wonderful and magical. I have seen it on the television as I think David Attenborough did something on it once in a wildlife programme, but I imagine it is truly awe-inspiring in real life.

Seeing the Falls one day is definitely on my bucket list.

Write soon,

Anna

p.s. Not sure 'bucket list' translates into Dutch – it just means a wish list of things to do before you die, i.e. 'kick the bucket' I presume (again, not sure how that will translate?).

Email from Dann to Anna

Hi Anna

Yes, the rain has been a bit on the biblical side recently.

The river got so high last week that Grace had to put the anti-crocodile nets up around the sunken fire pit at the Lodge. She doesn't want to lose any guests while they are enjoying a sunset braai. She said that would be very bad for trade!

I am glad Henry was inspired by Victoria Falls, they are truly epic. I have been there many times over the last five years, perhaps over twenty, in both the wet and the dry, and you just can't help but be utterly captivated by their awesome size and power. As you know, I am not a religious man but it does make you feel something spiritual when you stand next to the edge of the gorge and feel the roar of the water ringing in your ears and pounding in your chest.

I hope one day you can see it for yourself, and that you have no plans to kick any buckets in the foreseeable future?

Oh, and apologies from me – I let slip the other day to Grace that you and I were still writing to each other. She didn't say anything, just smiled that smile. Sorry.

Regards

Dann

Letter from Henry to Anna

Dear Miss Anna

Henry's word of the day: DIORAMA

Hope you like this photo from our trip to Mosi-oa-Tunya. Do you think we look funny in our big raincoats? It is hard to tell who is who because we all look the same, although Mr Huismann is the tallest so you can see him on the right. I am third from left – you can see my raincoat almost touches the floor. I hope you can see some of the waterfall in the background although it doesn't look as impressive in the photo as the real thing.

I meant to tell you about our trip to Livingstone Museum the same day. It is the largest and oldest museum in the whole of Zambia, so we are very proud of it. My favourite parts were the natural history galleries because there were lots of big displays showing Zambian animals, plants, frogs, fish and birds, and even a stuffed black mamba. Mr Tembo used the word I've chosen for today to describe the displays that I liked. I enjoyed the exhibit about David Livingstone too, which had lots of interesting photographs, and also the gallery about Zambia's history and the struggles that our nation went through before we became independent in 1964. Mr Tembo gave us each a clipboard and questions that we had to find the answers to from around the museum, which was fun to do. I was the only one to spot the two types of Lechwe antelopes which are unique to Zambia, so I got a gold star for my year book.

Love

Henry x

Letter from Anna to Henry

Dear Henry

Anna's word of the day: DIPLODOCUS

I did like your photo and I could certainly see how magnificent the Falls looked in the background.

Thank you for telling me about your visit to the museum too. Well done for your gold star!! I remember the first time I went to London was when I was about your age, and we visited the Natural History Museum. We also had to look for answers to questions when we went. I remember we were doing a project on dinosaurs. They used to have a massive skeleton of a huge plant-eating dinosaur in the entrance hall. He was affectionately called Dippy and was known all over the world. I remember thinking it was the most amazing thing I had ever seen. It's still my favourite museum and I visit it whenever I can.

One day, if you take a break from exploring and find yourself in London, I would definitely recommend a visit.

Love Anna x

February

Email from Grace to Anna

My dearest Anna

I am struggling to write this, but I feel I owe you a heartfelt apology.

I was sitting on my veranda yesterday when Dann appeared out of the blue. It was so warm and, I confess, I was daydreaming a bit. Since I have started to write to you, I have been remembering all the funny things that have happened to us here, like the time a huge male baboon swam across the river at low tide to Musanga Island. It nearly scared our guests half to death when it sauntered into the camp and, cool as you like, grabbed a watermelon from the fruit display which it clamped between its enormous teeth before promptly swimming back across the river to Zimbabwe!

Or the time a dead hippopotamus floated slowly by the Lodge, with its white belly turned upwards and a huge crocodile firmly attached to each leg. It was such a curious sight, Piet filmed it on his phone and teased the children that it was the Zambezi river god Nyami Nyami paying us a visit to make sure they were all behaving.

Anyway, I digress. Dann sat down on the big old sofa next to me and held my hand. He was frowning and there was some sadness in his eyes.

He was kind but quite firm when he said, 'Grace, you know how fond I am of you but I have never been blind to your schemes over the years. Even though I know you do it with all the best of intentions, I have to tell you your interference won't work this time. I know Anna and I have enjoyed writing to each other, and that you hoped something would come of it, but I have decided it is not fair to draw her into a friendship that will never be anything more. I'm going to write one last time to say I don't think it is a good idea if we continue to write. Better now for both of us than in the future.'

I said, 'Dann, has something happened? I've seen you happier these last few months than for the last five years. I know you are scared but perhaps now is the time,' but he just shook his head and said, 'I am not sure there will ever be a time, Grace.' He kissed my hand with affection, and then left as quickly as he had come.

I will never give up hope of finding him love, but I hope you will forgive me for my inexcusable interference. I found one of your earlier emails that said Emma Woodhouse was 'meddlesome' and I fear very much that is what I have been.

I do not know what has been in your heart these past months, but I am just hopeful that you saw this as a pleasant distraction, an interesting correspondence, and nothing more. I would never forgive myself if my interference has caused either of you long-lasting pain.

In my defence, perhaps it was because I know that, like

him, you have a kind soul, and he is so desperately in need of salvation. I had hoped you and he could find some sort of connection, but he has made me realise that these are just the foolish and fruitless wishes of an old romantic who should have known better. I have decided once and for all that my matchmaking days are over.

Please say my pride and hubris won't put you off corresponding with me, as I have so enjoyed our letters these last few months.

Kindest regards

Grace

Email from Anna to Grace

Dearest Grace

Thank you for your email. Please do not feel badly. As I wrote earlier, I was not, and am not, looking for any sort of relationship. I may be a singleton but I am a happy singleton – we do exist, you know! 😊

I can reassure you that writing to Dann has certainly been a pleasant distraction but nothing more. He seems like a genuine and sincere person and I am disappointed that he no longer feels he is able to write to me as a friend, but I perfectly respect his wishes and I can assure you that my heart is not broken.

I will of course keep writing to you and, I hope, you to me, and to Henry of course. I have loved our letters, and hearing about your country, home and school have been truly inspirational.

Best wishes

Anna

Hey sis

Just forwarding on this email from Grace Nkomo about Dann. I wonder why he no longer wants to write to me? It is so out of the blue.

I thought we were getting on quite well for two people who have never met (works for people on the internet all the time). I have to say I feel a bit disappointed. Not naïve enough to think we were ever going to be the new Burton and Taylor, and he never pledged any feelings for me, but he seemed kind and funny.

Oh God, perhaps I am missing Matt more than I want to admit and was projecting my loneliness onto the first half-decent man who had the misfortune to come into view.

I wonder what Grace means by 'desperately in need of salvation'? I googled it – it means 'deliverance from guilt'!

Love A xx

p.s. Should I write to Dann one last time?

Email from Izzy to Anna

Hey little sis

Like every reality show we've ever watched, in no particular order:

1. You're not missing Matt, you're just feeling sorry for yourself. He's a first-class loser and if you ever have him back in your life I will disown you.
2. You feel sad because you liked Dann, but it will pass.

Remember your unrequited love for Gary Holt at junior school?

3. If you still feel blue, try prosecco, chocolate or ice-cream, or all three at the same time (in moderation).

4. Anyway, if you had got together, I would have been forced to call you DAnna (aka Brangelina) and you would never forgive me for that.

5. Perhaps one last letter would be okay, but don't come over as lonely and/or desperate – men hate those things.

6. Agree, salvation is an interesting word, I wonder why she used it? You said his wife and child had died in a car crash but perhaps he murdered them!

Did this help? (Not the last one, that was flippant and in poor taste.)

Izzy x

Email from Dann to Femke Huismann

Hallo mama

Ik weet dat ik zei dat ik iemand had ontmoet, maar het is niet gelukt. Sorry. Liefs voor jou en papa.

Dann xx

Email from Dann to Anna

Dear Anna

I hope you are well.

I found myself hesitating before starting this email – in fact, I've been staring at the blank screen for at least ten minutes.

I hope you know I have enjoyed writing to you and receiving your letters and emails but I wanted to let you know that I don't think I will have time to write again. I am so busy at the school, with all the after-school activities I run, and with getting the Arts Centre built and ready to open, I am struggling to find enough hours in the day for anything else. I didn't want to be a bad friend and just stop writing without an explanation.

I know Henry and Grace love hearing from you and sharing their news from here, so I am sure you will continue to write to them.

Thank you for being my pen-pal, even if it was only for a short while. I have enjoyed it very much.

Wishing you peace and happiness.

Dann

Email from Anna to Izzy

Hey

I was just going to draft an email to Dann when this arrived. Given what Grace said he told her, I know it isn't about him just being too busy to write, but never mind, seems my days as a thirty-five-year-old pen-pal are officially over. What was I thinking!

Love Anna

BTW, I've got an email in my inbox from Matt. I haven't opened it. I know your views. Should I see what he wants?

Love

Anna x

Hey

Disappointed about you and the dishy Dutchman, I had a bit of a tingle about you two but I may just be getting a cold.

Definitely don't open the email from Matt, he will want something and you are too soft and will give in, whatever it is.

Forward it to me and I will reply for you (I'll blind copy you in). Don't worry, despite my ill-concealed loathing for the Ratt, I will be nice and wholly appropriate. I told you I am doing quite well learning the art of diplomacy.

Love Izzy

Email from Izzy to Matthew Tanner, copied to Anna

Hello Matt

How absolutely lovely to hear from you.

Sorry I am replying on behalf of Anna, but she is just about to jet off for an extended luxury trip to Africa and I am looking after her inbox while she is 'off-grid'. She's taken up white-water rafting and the rapids of the Zambezi are a must-do for any aspiring paddler. She's going with her new man – has she mentioned him? He is ex-Special Forces, I think, and certainly has the muscles for it.

Sorry to hear that you and Gretchen have split up. That

is truly terrible news but I will, of course, let Anna know as soon as she is back in the country, perhaps in two or three months. However, I suspect she will have little time to send her own condolences given how busy she is.

Do keep in touch.

With very best wishes,

Izzy

Email from Anna to Izzy

OMG Izzy. What did you say that for?! He'll never believe I'm going to Africa. What if he contacts Ellie? Worse, knowing my absolute loathing for adrenaline sports, he definitely won't believe I've suddenly taken up white-water rafting. I think I once told him I would rather poke out my eyes with a stick than ever do anything so stupid.

And where on earth would I have met a muscly member of the SAS – in Liberty's fabric section??

If I could find an 'exasperated' emoji, I'd attach it here!

Anna x

Email from Izzy to Anna

Well, I thought it was imaginative and inspired, but no need to thank me.

Why write and tell you about him and Miss Stick splitting up? I can only think of one or two reasons why he would even bother contacting you, and neither would be positive for you.

He'll never know you aren't going to Africa. And, thinking about it, have you thought about going to visit Grace for a nice luxury break? You love all that nature stuff and are always saying how amazing she makes it sound. I can't remember the last time you had a proper holiday so it would do you good... and you never know, being close to a certain teacher might make him change his mind about wanting to know you better.

Love

Izzy x

Email from Anna to Izzy

Hmmm...

March

Dearest Anna

I just had to write to tell you our wonderful news.

As of yesterday, our new Women's Community Arts Centre is officially finished. Dann told me he had written to tell you about it in one of his emails.

I met with some of the women from the village last week and, after much deliberation, we have decided to call it 'Twalumba', which you may translate as 'We are thankful' … and we certainly are.

I know I am biased but it looks splendid, and I am so proud of what everyone has achieved. There has been so much hard work over the last year, from the labourers who built it from the very first block up, to the tradesmen who have installed the water pump and the generator, and to everyone in the village, at the school and at Baobab Tree Lodge who have brought in equipment that they have so generously purchased, recycled or donated.

It reminded me of opening Mwabonwa and the hard work we did so long ago. I even helped to make some of the curtains, which really took me back, although my fingers aren't as nimble as they used to be and I find I can only work my sewing machine for an hour or so at a time now.

We hope to have a small opening ceremony soon and I will be sure to take some photographs to send to you. I am also going to ask Esther to put out a call on our website for volunteers from among our supporters who can perhaps come and teach the women some of the advanced skills they will need. Many are already excellent seamstresses but they are all self-taught and would so benefit from learning more about their craft. We often have university students come from all over the world for a term or two as part of their studies, so I am sure we can find some suitable tutors among that cohort.

I will write again soon with photos.

Love Grace

Email from Esther to Anna

Dear Miss Anna

Please don't tell Grace I have sent you this message, as she would be cross with me. I know she has written to you about how we are shortly due to open Twalumba and that we will need to find some instructors.

When we were speaking about it last week, Grace said, 'Wouldn't it be wonderful if Anna was able to come for a short while? She is so talented and artistic, I know she would make a very knowledgeable teacher.'

I said, 'Miss Grace, why don't you ask her to come?' but she said, 'I can't do that. She has her own life and business to run over in London, she would never have the time and I would hate to embarrass her by asking and her having to turn me down.'

Well, I am not too embarrassed to ask you and will not be offended if you turn me down.

Would you come, Miss Anna? I know Grace would love to meet you as she speaks so highly of you. I am sure if you said yes we could find you a nice room at the Lodge. There are always one or two spare that do not quite meet our guest standard and are waiting for refurbishment but are perfectly serviceable.

If you say yes, she will be angry with me for a while for going behind her back, but not for long I am sure, and nothing I cannot bear.

I await your reply.

With kindest regards

Esther (Ng'andu)

Email from Anna to Grace

Dear Grace

I hope you are all well there at Baobab Tree Lodge.

It was great news to hear about the progress on Twalumba Women's Art Centre – you must be very proud that it is nearly ready to welcome the local women. I can't wait to see your photographs.

I was interested in your comment about volunteer design and craft tutors so looked at your website for more details. I hope I am not being too presumptuous, but I wonder if it would be okay for me to be one of your volunteers and come over to help out at Twalumba for a short while?

My spring designs are ready to go so I'm at something of a loose end. I have a talented production team here and a very accomplished office manager called Eleanor (she is my Esther!) who is more than happy to manage the day-to-day running of the business if I'm absent for a while. I could be available for three or four months, say from April until early July, if that would be acceptable.

I am not sure if my visit would even be feasible, as I would require some accommodation to be provided, but I have to say you would be doing me a great honour. I have been so inspired by your stories and vivid descriptions of your home that I would love to meet you in person, and Henry too, and see your wonderful lodge, school and country for myself. Perhaps I am more like Mrs Molloy than I thought and am ready to embrace a new challenge.

As you can see, I am being entirely selfish, so do hope you will say yes.

I look forward to hearing from you.

Kindest regards

Anna x

Email from Grace to Anna

Dearest Anna

I was overjoyed to receive your email. We will be delighted to have someone with your knowledge, experience and expertise at Twalumba for a few months, as will the local women. On a personal note, I will be thrilled to welcome you to my home and our wonderful country for the first time. I know you will not be disappointed.

Esther eventually confessed that she had asked you to come, but I am too happy and excited to be cross with her. She said she mentioned there may be accommodation available at the Lodge but all our rooms are currently booked. However, I do have Cottage No. 10 free until early July – I hope that will be as good (better I think!) for you? I actually think it has one of the best uninterrupted views across the river as it stands at the widest part of the bend on the furthest eastern edge of our property. It has a small piece of land adjacent to it that I have decided to enhance by building a private plunge pool for next season's guests, which is why it is unoccupied and available now.

There may be workmen there on occasion while you are here, but they will only be working outside, and there is still a very pretty, secluded and private deck out across the water that you can use. The sunsets from that end of the property are magical too and, if you care for it, you won't find a prettier spot to spend time watching the abundant bird life that calls the Zambezi home. If I ever lost Samuel for a few hours and the boat was still at the jetty, I could guarantee he would be at that end of the property with his bird books and binoculars.

I hope this sounds suitable?

When you know, please email me with details of your flight and I will make sure someone from the Lodge is at the airport to meet you.

With kindest regards

Grace

Dearest Anna

I completely forgot to tell you in all the excitement about the Centre that I have other important news to share.

I've just heard that Dr Lund is coming back to Mwabonwa soon to continue her research and will be with us for at least six months. I know I shouldn't interfere (again!!) but this time I am very hopeful of good things to come for her and Dann when they are living side by side once more. I will try to see what magical spells I can cast, hopefully without him noticing until it is too late for him to resist. When you come, I would be interested in your view on them as a potential love match. I am sure you will agree what an attractive and compatible couple they make.

I know I told you my matchmaking days were over but I just can't give up on him, so perhaps, one day soon, I will be able to place an order for one of your wedding hats after all!

I will write with any developments before you arrive.

Best regards

Grace

Email from Anna to Ellie

Morning Ellie

Hope you had a lovely weekend.

I'm running a bit late, should be with you about ten. Are you free for a chat when I get in? I have a bit of a wild plan that I want to tell you about but I will need your help to achieve it. Will explain more when I get there, but it involves me going to Africa for a while!

See you shortly,

Anna x

Email from Henry to Anna (via Chabota)

Dear Miss Anna

Mr Munyama has given me special permission to email this from the IT classroom, as I said it will take too much time to write and I couldn't wait any longer. Our IT Technician Chabota has very kindly let me use his email and is going to press 'Send' when I have finished. I am finding typing much harder than writing a letter. I keep forgetting where all the letters are.

Mama Grace has just told me you are coming to stay at Baobab in April to teach at Twalumba. I am so excited I can't stop jumping up and down.

You will be able to see my school and meet my family and talk to my teachers and teach me how to play chess and show my mother how to design fabric and eat my daddy's food.

Please let me know what date you will be arriving, so I can count down the days.

Love Henry x

Email from Anna to Grace

Dear Grace

I cannot tell you how much I am looking forward to coming,

and thank you, the cottage sounds ideal.

I am getting the overnight flight from London down to Johannesburg on the 4th April, then picking up the connecting flight back up to Zambia so, delays notwithstanding, should be arriving into Livingstone Airport at about 3 o'clock on the afternoon on the 5th April.

I will of course let you know if any of my plans change but if not, I very much look forward to meeting you on the 5th.

Kindest regards

Anna x

Email from Anna to Izzy

Hi sis

Hope all well with the clan.

Big news. I know it may feel like karma or fate or whatever, after what you told Matt, and don't think I've gone completely mad, but I am going to Zambia for three months! Not for a holiday though. Grace Nkomo wrote to tell me about their new Women's Art Centre and how they were looking for helpers to teach art and design, so I've volunteered.

Ellie is very happy to have the extra responsibility at the shop. I know she feels she is ready for it so has jumped at the challenge.

I've booked my flights. I leave on the 4th April.

Anna x

Email from Izzy to Anna

OMG!

I know what I said but WOW, I didn't actually expect you to take me seriously! I'm not altogether surprised though and they will be lucky to have you. Perhaps you will come back with some inspiration for a new African collection – animal prints and exotic feathers? Anyway, how exciting. Keep me posted about your travel plans as I will worry.

Love

Izzy x

p.s. BTW, no need to thank me for my inspired idea, which I seem to remember at the time you wholeheartedly pooh-poohed!

p.p.s. What about my other brilliant suggestion? Any thoughts of rekindling your friendship with a certain dishy Dutchman?

Email from Anna to Izzy

Hey

A big fat definite NO ref. Dann Huismann – that boat has sailed, if indeed a boat actually even existed in the first place.

Anyway, Grace has turned her matchmaking gaze back towards Dr Lund, who is returning to Mwabonwa soon. She says Lottie and Dann have loads in common and make a very handsome couple, so are in all ways a much more suitable match. Oh, and she saw them kissing last time

Lottie was there, so it seems like Grace will be pushing at an open door. Anyway, didn't I tell you I was off men?

My focus is 100% on the ladies at Twalumba. I can't wait to meet Henry and Grace and to teach the local women some new skills to help them with their businesses. Excited and slightly trepedatious (suspect that's not even a proper word!) at the same time.

Speak before I go.

Love Anna x

✻

Email from Izzy to Anna

Hey

Just checking you are all ready for the start of your big adventure tomorrow. Got everything you need?

Izzy xx

p.s. Don't forget your paperwork and your anti-malaria tablets!

Email from Anna to Izzy

Hey back

Yes, I think I'm good to go. You know me, the queen of lists.

Passport, visa and Malarone – all check.

I'll drop you an email as soon as I get there.

Wish me luck!

Love Anna xx

Part Two

IN ZAMBIA

April

Hey

Just arrived at the Lodge. I'll get unpacked and then send you more news.

Love Anna

(Oh, it is beautiful here!!)

Email from Anna to Izzy

Hi

Me again, just finished getting everything away so thought I would give you a quick update, but will write again over the next few days as I settle in.

I am tired but also buzzing a bit now that I am actually here! I think just the act of travelling knocked my stuffing out a bit but at least there isn't a big time difference travelling north to south rather than east to west, so no jet lag to speak of. I am sure I will feel as right as rain after a good night's sleep.

The flights were fine and, thank goodness, all on time. Managed to get some sleep on the overnight plane down to Johannesburg, and then caught the shuttle back up to Livingstone. I think it was sixteen hours from walking up the steps on to the plane at Heathrow to walking into the terminal building here, which wasn't bad.

Livingstone Airport is charming and very small – no massive concourses to negotiate thankfully. We just walked off the plane, across the tarmac and into the terminal, through passport control (the stern-looking border official in the booth spent a long time looking at my paperwork, which was a bit alarming, but my visa was all good in the end) and then into a small but airy hall.

Five minutes later, a man came along on a little electric buggy with a cage on the back full of our luggage, which he then just stacked in the middle of the floor. Do you remember the last time we landed back at Gatwick from that girls' weekend in Barcelona? It took us two hours to get through passport control and another one to get our luggage!

The arrivals hall is so small that the people waiting to greet passengers are just off to one side behind a small barrier. I had been a bit worried about what I would do if no one was there to meet me but I needn't have been. I recognised Dann straightaway (he is taller than I thought), with a very pretty blonde lady who I now know is Dr Lund, and little Henry too, frantically waving a huge home-made banner that was almost as big as he is, that read 'Welcome to Miss Anna Peel'.

I got my luggage and then we all said hello and shook

hands a bit awkwardly. Dann took my bags and little Henry gripped my hand and I don't think let go until we got to the Lodge. Their minibus was right outside the terminal so we were on our way in less than ten minutes.

My very first impressions of Livingstone is that it is bustling and bright and hot and dusty and noisy. There were lots of people milling about and cars and mopeds jockeying for position and honking their horns, trying to get the prime spots outside the terminal. There was a man selling pineapples and bottles of water just outside the door and a few tour companies holding up signs saying things like 'Visit Victoria Falls', 'Accommodation for all pockets' and 'See the Big Five here'. The main road out of Livingstone was packed with small shops and stalls. Some had wonderful and baffling names, like 'Rise Again Funeral Directors and Bakery'! Do you think they started in funerals and then went into baking, or vice versa?

I sat in the back with Henry, and Lottie upfront with Dann. Henry didn't stop talking for the whole journey but he is absolutely delightful. Dann asked if I had a good flight and some other pleasantries but seemed more interested in keeping his eyes on the road to avoid the potholes as you leave town. We passed the armed check-point into the national park, as Henry described from his visit to the Falls. He was right, those guys are scary, but they didn't even seem to notice our van. Dann said they are mostly looking for poachers and smugglers, and a Lodge minibus with three white people and a small child in it is of absolutely no interest to them.

A few miles further on, there was a small roadside sign that said 'Baobab Tree Lodge and Mwabonwa School' and an arrow pointing left. We took the turning and then bumped our way down a very rutted dirt road for about another two miles.

As we got near, there was a sign to the school on the right and, a little further again, another sign for the Lodge.

I have to say, as we pulled into it I was a bit underwhelmed. There was a dusty roundabout and some car ports to one side, and just a long, low black roof at ankle level.

But, Izzy, when I walked down the steps into the open-sided Reception, what a magical sight! The property falls away in a series of steps down towards the main buildings and lawns, with boardwalks scooting this way and that. Right outside Reception, there was a small family of vervet monkeys, like Chutu, just sitting on the low branch of a tree grooming each other, their tails swinging beneath them like furry metronomes. Just beyond the very stylish buildings and some large shady trees, I got my first sight of the mighty Zambezi glinting in the sun.

I don't know what to say about the Zambezi except it is absolutely beautiful and magnificent. The Lodge sits on one side of a large bend in the river so you can see a huge expanse of water as it flows downstream. I feel like I have arrived in a magical lost world.

Grace and Esther were in Reception to meet us. We hugged like we were long lost friends. They are both lovely. I have been invited over for tea tomorrow afternoon when I have settled in, so I will email again later.

Love

Anna x

Email from Izzy to Anna

Hi sis

Great to hear you arrived in one piece. The Lodge sounds lovely – now tell me more about Dann!

    Izzy xx

    p.s. Only joking, it all sounds amazing. Tell me all about it when you have time.

❖

Email from Anna to Izzy

Morning sis, from beautiful Zambia.

I had a great night's sleep, so am full of beans this morning. One of my first impressions - it's so dark here at night! I've spent so many years used to 'London darkness' meaning a dirty orange glow in the sky, it is a bit disconcerting when the lights are off and there is just a deep inky blackness that you can almost touch. There are also a lot of sounds that are unfamiliar: the whirring of cicadas and the croaking of frogs. Anyway, I was so tired after travelling, even the other worldliness of it all couldn't stop me, and I was out like a light before I knew it. I didn't stir until it was quite bright outside and I am now sitting on my little porch drinking tea.

    My cottage is lovely. It's the end building of a number of similar guest suites along one of the raised boardwalks that criss-cross the whole property. Grace said the grass can get very wet and spongy during the rainy season so they keep everyone's feet dry.

My cottage is very small, really just a roundel with a thatched roof, a big bed complete with a mosquito net, a small wardrobe and drawers, and a tiny bathroom. I love the decoration though – lots of African prints and colourful rugs. Outside there is a covered porch (where I am typing this), like an open-air living area, with a big comfy sofa and coffee table. Oh, and I have an outside shower… that may take some getting used to!

I don't have a kitchen but I do have a kettle, a fridge, and crockery and cutlery. As I am here for a while, Grace has also kindly installed a small microwave for me. She has said that if I want any supplies, I can just pop into the Lodge kitchen or Reception for tea, coffee etc, and for dinner, I can choose whatever I like from that day's menu and one of the chefs will box it up ready for me to collect later in the day.

From where I'm sitting, I can see the Zambezi sparkling just a few feet away. I've got a small private decking area that stretches out over the river by ten feet or so, with a small bistro table and two chairs. Grace was right, the view of the Zambezi from my cottage is spectacular. On the other side of the building, Grace is having a small plunge pool built for next year's guests (which is why I am able to use the cottage during my stay) and the two lovely builders, Francis and Victor, have just been around to introduce themselves and to say they hope they won't be too noisy. I can't see them from my side of the cottage, and they can't see me from theirs, so I am fairly sure I can use my outside shower without any concern.

I am going to do some aimless exploring this morning

while everyone is at church and then I'm off to take tea with Grace this afternoon, which sounds very civilised.

Love

Anna x

Email from Anna to Izzy

Hi

I had a very enjoyable afternoon taking tea with Grace. She is really wonderful. I think she would best be described as a force of nature! It is quite strange, though, meeting someone for the first time who you think you already know so well and are so fond of. She has certainly made me feel extremely welcome.

Dann popped over for a cuppa too, which was nice. Grace speaks to him affectionately, and he to her. They seem to have a special bond and are obviously very close. He certainly smiles more in her direction than at anyone else I have seen so far.

I have to say, the Lodge is amazing and much grander than I imagined. It is a large white colonial-style building with a deep portico to the front held up by fluted white columns. Grace has the west wing as her private quarters, for herself and her housekeeper Sarah. She certainly has impeccable taste; it is beautifully furnished.

The rest of the Lodge is given over to guest accommodation and some public spaces, like the library. Grace laughed when she said that, while all her visitors like the thought of being in the African bush, some of them are actually a bit nervous of the bugs and spiders so prefer their rooms with floors and walls that meet, rather than rooms like my little cottage, which has gaps all over the place for creepy-crawlies to get in (none seen yet though!).

There is also a magnificently manicured lawn that stretches down from the building to the riverbank jetty, dotted with colourful tended flowerbeds, so different from the native bush that surrounds the rest of the property. Grace says her garden is her one indulgence now and it certainly is beautiful.

Love

Anna x

Email from Izzy to Anna

And??

Email from Anna to Izzy

And what?

Email from Izzy to Anna

I know you are being deliberately obtuse, stop it. Don't make me ask three times!

Email from Anna to Izzy

Not sure what you want me to say. I like his accent. He seems quiet and reserved but has an easy charm that is quite appealing. Perhaps a bit distant. From my limited time speaking with him since I arrived, he's perfectly pleasant, but I don't detect any of that connection we had when we first wrote to each other.

Enough?

For now. When do you think you'll start work at the centre?

Hi sis

Hopefully tomorrow!

Before she went to church, Grace asked me when I would like to see the Arts Centre, so I said as soon as possible – it's the reason I'm here after all. So we went over straight after we'd finished our tea. She had made some phone calls earlier and said a few of the women would be there to meet me and say hello.

The actual building is very simple, just a long rectangular shape with a small toilet block to one side, two sinks in a covered porchway and a water standpipe. There's a basic food preparation area inside but the rest of the space is taken up with large work tables, sewing machines, cupboards and shelving. The windows have no glass but do have curtains, and the roof overhangs a long way, which is common here, to keep out the rain and the sun equally. At one end of the room is a blackboard and a large noticeboard. So far the only things on the noticeboard are the hat sketches I sent to Grace. She said she hoped I didn't mind, which of course I don't, but that they made the bare room look very creative and stylish and she hopes they will give the ladies inspiration.

Grace said the local women have decided that they want to manage the day-to-day running of the Centre, not just use its facility, so they have already set up a small group called the Twalumba Ladies Co-operative. Grace says she is glad I am here, though, because I've run a business and she's a bit worried the ladies may have bitten off more than they can chew! There is a lot to do – not just the creative work, but they will need to appoint a caretaker and someone to look after stock and the finances, as well as devising teaching rotas and class timetables, staff and volunteer welfare, human resources, general admin etc etc. I said I didn't want to step on anyone's toes, but Grace said there is no office politics or ladder-climbing here, which is refreshing. She has already told them I will be able to help them with the many tasks they have to do, and they are apparently all looking forward to my guidance.

The three ladies who make up the organising committee – Joyce Chibwe, Thelma Musonda and Patience Sitali – were at the Centre to welcome me. They are all from the local village and seemed genuinely delighted to have me there. They each shook my hand and Joyce said, 'Miss Anna, we have heard so much about you, you are so famous. We are very happy to have you join us.'

Joyce is about fifty, I would say, and very small and round with an infectious smile. Her five children are all grown up and live nearby. She already has fourteen grandchildren and two more on the way. Thelma is a spinster. She is quieter and slightly younger than Joyce and is apparently an excellent dressmaker. And Patience is the youngest of the trio. She has two small children – her youngest son, Innocent, who is only eight weeks old, was strapped to her back as is the custom here, and her older son is in the Tiny Tots Reception class at Mwabonwa.

The Twalumba Ladies gave me a guided tour of the facility. The first task is to get in all the stock that they will need. Esther from the Lodge has been helping them set up as she is very organised and is a great administrator, so orders have already been placed for a number of bolts of fabric and other necessities. There is apparently a very good stockist in Livingstone that is happy to provide as much of the sewing equipment and art supplies as we need, and Grace has already gifted them a generous amount of money to cover all our purchases until the Twalumba Ladies' fundraising activities and sales start to generate money and they can become self-sufficient.

Joyce, Thelma and Patience have asked all the women they know who want to come to the Centre what they want to learn and they have said that as well as sewing, they would like to try fabric design, cloth dyeing, quilting, knitting and other crafts like basket-making and beadwork. I said I can happily teach the first five but the basket-making and beadwork will have to be a joint voyage of discovery, so I am very happy for us to all learn together.

The Twalumba Ladies seemed very happy with that response. They asked if I would like to be the fourth member of the Twalumba Ladies Co-operative organising committee. I said, 'As long as you're sure,' and their enthusiastic nodding meant I have been readily accepted, at least for the few months I am here.

Izzy, it is quite daunting but also very exciting. There is so much to do, and so many people will be looking to me for help, but I can't wait to get started. So, as of tomorrow morning, I will officially be one of the Twalumba Women's Art Centre teaching team (in truth, so far, I think that is just me!) and a temporary member of the Twalumba Ladies Co-operative.

I've suggested to Joyce, Thelma and Patience that, first thing tomorrow, all four of us should sit down and draw up a timetable of classes that we can advertise locally. The Centre doesn't open until about 11 o'clock so that should give us an early head start. The good news is that Grace says that we have two student volunteers starting a week on Monday until September. Matilde is studying Art and Fabric Design in Paris, and Carolina is from Portugal, studying English and Textiles. I have a feeling they will be extremely busy when they arrive.

I'll let you know how I get on.

Love Anna x

✿

Email from Anna to Izzy

Hey sis

Just back from my first day at Twalumba. I haven't run around so much in ages, my feet are aching and my back is singing a bit, but it has been really rewarding and much better than I could ever have imagined.

Grace is so thoughtful. When I got back to my cottage, I found a bottle of local angelica root gin on the doorstep with a note that said 'To celebrate your first day at Twalumba.

Tonic, ice and lemon in your fridge, love Grace xx'. So, I had a quick shower, poured myself a drink (a very small one – I am working tomorrow!) and am relaxing on my outside sofa with my tired, swollen feet up on the coffee table. BTW, showering outside is very liberating!

I was up at the Centre early today, just before 8 o'clock, but Joyce was already opening up so we had a chance to chat for a while. As the oldest, Joyce is obviously the matriarch of the trio and was surprisingly candid, saying that they haven't been very organised since they opened. She said a lot of women have popped in and started one or two projects, and more come every day, but there hasn't been much direction or guidance. She took my hand and said, 'We are so glad to have you Miss Anna, truly,' which was lovely. I just hope I don't let anyone down.

When Thelma and Patience arrived just after nine, Joyce and I already had a big pot of tea brewing and some note pads, pens and post-it notes laid out on the big cutting table, as well as sheets of flipchart paper, blu-tack and marker pens. I said, 'Let's spend an hour or so brainstorming before the first ladies arrive.' I had to explain what I meant as it wasn't a term any of them had heard before, but once they realised that they could say or suggest anything, however off-the-wall, they came up with some amazing ideas.

We were all in agreement that what we don't want to do is patronise the women who come here. Even though many of them have little or no formal education, they all have the same thing in common: they want to learn. We've decided, therefore, how important it is to make sure there is a good variety of classes and levels for everyone.

So, as of today, we have drawn up a very rudimentary

timetable of classes we could offer, although I expect it will take quite a lot of tweaking before we get it exactly right. I feel sorry for our poor students Matilde and Carolina, who start next week, as we have already created twice-weekly teaching sessions for them in 'Dress Pattern Making' and 'Batik and the Hot Wax Principle of Dyeing'. Once they have started, and we get to know what areas of interest they have, I am sure we can pull together even more lessons for them to teach.

To start with, I am going to teach 'Knitting for beginners', 'Getting the most out of your sewing machine' and 'Fabric Design', as well as 'The Principles of Art and Drawing' for any of the ladies who want to be extra creative in other mediums.

Thelma has decided she would like to lead on 'Dress Making' for beginners, and at intermediate and advanced level, and Patience is going to help her, perhaps concentrating on children's clothes. Joyce is going to get creative with fabric gifts and homewares, like cushions and tablecloths.

We have also created two sessions called 'Learn together – Basket Weaving' and 'Learn together – Beadwork' as none of us know much about these crafts but are happy to work it out together as we go along. How hard can it be? Thelma says her friend, who is a fisherman, would be happy to collect local reeds for us to start weaving, and we think making our own painted beads should be quite simple. I am going to visit Mr Nkoso, to see if he can order me one or two books on the subject to start our own basic reference library, but I am glad that I can get online here quite easily and will ask Esther if she is happy to print off some how-to guides in the office for me.

There are already quite a lot of supplies in the Centre,

but we also made a wish-list of everything we would like, not just for our sewing projects but also art materials, wax, fabric dyes, batik cantings, paints, brushes, pencils and canvasses as well as coloured paper, glue and scissors. I hope Grace doesn't baulk at the initial cost, which I know she won't, but just in case, I am sure I can put together a good business case for selling some of our products in the Lodge shop to start to repay her generosity.

When the first ladies started to arrive, I was formally introduced by Joyce and shook a lot of hands. They are all ages and from all parts of the district. Some of the women are very young, often with babies who they carry on their backs. Mostly you can just see the tops of their heads and their chubby legs sticking out of their traditional slings.

We told them some of our plans but did say it would probably take a few weeks to get everything working smoothly. I didn't want to raise their expectations but no one seemed to mind. There was just a lot of excitement and happy chatter and laughter, which was very infectious.

I know they say hard work and reward go hand-in-hand, and that is certainly how I feel after today. I know it is only day one but the centre has such potential for the women of the area. A lady called Enid, who has three small children, asked if we could set up a creche. I just said 'everything is possible' so I am going to think about how that could work in practice.

And I can honestly say, a G&T has never ever tasted so good!

Hope all well at home.

Write soon. Love Anna x

Stuck late in the office drafting an urgent report on burglary trends (dull!) but that's a splendid idea - the gin is coming out as soon as I get home! And I love that your head is buzzing with creative ideas, I haven't heard you this excited or enthused for ages!

Love

Izzy xx

❈

Hi

Just back from Henry's so thought I would write before bed. It is still warm and has been quite dry today, so I am sitting outside on my covered porch to type.

There was a note under my door earlier from Harold, asking if I would like to go to their house for dinner. He says that it is traditional to welcome visitors with food, however humble, and as it is his day off from the Lodge, he was going to cook a traditional Zambian feast. He invited Dann and Lottie too, and Grace, although she has unfortunately had to decline due to a commitment at her church.

It was a lovely evening. Harold is definitely as good a cook as he is a gardener.

Henry had told me so much about their house, which makes up part of the old school building, and it was so nice to see it for the first time. It is quite small, particularly for a family of seven, and simply furnished but extremely welcoming and Hester keeps it spotless. There was a small painted wooden sign hanging by a piece of wire from the doorknob of Harold and Hester's bedroom that read 'DO NOT DISTURB'. Harold said, 'In such a small house, how else would we get any privacy to make so many beautiful babies?' which made us all laugh.

The house is too small for everyone to eat inside so Grace had lent them two tables and tablecloths from the Lodge, which they had set up in the yard, and also some fairy lights that had been strung between the trees. Henry says the chickens normally roam free but Milimo had locked them away in their coop for the night in case having them pecking around our feet bothered us. Similarly, their yard dog had been tied up behind the house. She doesn't have a name – they call her Mubwa, which I think just means dog. They say she is friendly but she looked quite menacing, so I was glad about that. She is not a pet – her main job is to warn the family about snakes!

I am sure the children don't see their yard looking so magical very often. The babies Harriet and Hannah were very quiet and spent much of the evening just gurgling and staring up at the coloured lights as if it was Christmas. At one point, Harriet crawled over and Dann picked her up and she promptly settled down on his lap and went to sleep. Hester said, 'Dann, you are a natural,' but I was in conversation with Lottie at the time so didn't hear what he said in response.

Harold's kitchen at home isn't very large either, so he had prepared the meal at the Lodge and brought it home with him. I have to say it was all delicious, and completely new to me in terms of flavours. We had traditional nshima (unique here so hard to describe, but I would say something like polenta) with stewed okra, pumpkin and sweet potatoes, goat meat that had been on Grace's slow barbecue all day, and chikanda. I wasn't sure what the last one was. It looked a bit like meatloaf but Harold says it is made from vegetables, peanuts and chilli. It was absolutely delicious but quite spicy.

We were all glad when Harold said he had decided against one of his own favourite delicacies, ifinkubala caterpillars, which he stews with tomatoes and onions. He is very widely travelled so knows that Europeans like us are quite squeamish when it comes to eating bugs. He said the children particularly like to snack on deep fried flying insects, which they call inswa, when they are in season. I said I would have been happy to try the flying bugs if he had any there (which he didn't!) but would probably draw the line at caterpillars, which made him laugh.

Harold is a really lovely man. He is like a big bear, quite stocky and rotund, but with easily the biggest smile of anyone I have ever met. He laughs a lot and seems to adore his family. The twins Milimo and Mabel seemed quite shy, but then aren't most teenagers around strangers? Hester is even more beautiful than in her photograph. She is so captivatingly lovely that I couldn't quite take my eyes off her. I know that if she was walking down the Old Kent Road, one of the local modelling agencies would have snapped her up. It helps that she is easily six feet tall and towers well above Harold.

It was nice to spend some time with Dann and Lottie as well. He doesn't say much about himself but is very interested in others and seemed genuinely fascinated when I told him more about our family of police officers. I expect he continues to wonder why I make hats when the rest of you are such fine, upstanding public servants, but he was far too polite to pry further.

Dr Lottie is very pretty, quite quiet and reserved. She seemed a little awkward in company. I think that may be the case with a lot of very clever people who live their lives in the solitary and rarefied atmosphere of academia. I asked her what her current research was about and then sort of wished I hadn't when she said, 'Tectonic movement in the early Cretaceous period and the interaction between sedimentary substances and basalt deposits'. She did have the good grace to smile when she could see I didn't really know what that meant. She said most people don't, which is why it is nice to have Dann at the school as a fellow geologist, so she has an 'intellectual equal'. I wasn't offended lol!

I can see why Grace thinks they make a handsome couple and are so compatible. Oh, did I tell you, he has cut his beard! Not completely, but it is now quite short and much neater, and he looks a bit less like a man of the woods. I suspect Grace made him trim it before Lottie arrived – she is obviously keen for him to make a good impression. I can see what Grace means about thinking him nice looking, although I would say his face is more interesting than conventionally handsome.

After the meal, Hester, Harold and the older twins sang us some beautiful local songs, which was captivating. It was the most perfect way to end a perfect evening. I feel incredibly welcomed to this lovely country by these gracious people.

Love

Anna x

Hey

We did a straw poll around the dinner table last night. Tom and Belle would have eaten the caterpillars. I didn't have the heart to tell Belle that it didn't really fit in with her vegan aspirations! I was with you. I think I could have managed the ant-things but the thought of squidgy caterpillar juices running down my throat made me feel a bit nauseous. Not surprisingly for a nine and a seven-year-old, Freddie and Georgia just went 'yuk yuk yuk'. 😊

Izzy xx

Email from Anna to Izzy

Oh, meant to say, off to Victoria Falls a week on Friday with a group of fourteen-year-olds. They are short of an appropriate adult to help out, so I jumped at the chance. I'll let you know what it's like when I get back.

Love

Anna x

✢

Email from Anna to Izzy

Hi sis

Back from my morning at Victoria Falls. Not sure what to say but am going to steal some of the words little Henry picked after his first visit: awe-inspiring, overwhelming, humbling and majestic!

It is a perfect time of year to visit. We are nearing the end of the rainy season but there was no rain today, so we had the best of both worlds – warm and dry but with the Zambezi still in full flood for maximum 'wow' factor. It was quite busy with tourists, which isn't surprising, it is the main reason people travel here from all over the world. Once you're inside the Falls park though, you don't feel crowded.

I took some photos, which I've attached, but they just don't do it justice. You just can't capture the sheer scale of it or the noise of the water, which is incredible and deafening.

The children were all very excited, and I think Dann was just thankful to have another responsible adult on hand to shepherd them around. Mr Tembo normally comes on these visits but he had to go to Kitwe to visit his poorly mum, so Dann would have had to cancel if I hadn't offered to help as everyone else was busy. He is good at shouting at the children if they are doing anything silly or dangerous, like trying to climb on the barriers to get a better look (his military bark is much worse than his bite!), but even so, some extra support was useful.

I loved driving through Livingstone on the way to the falls too, it is so vibrant and busy and colourful. I am not sure any of the drivers here have heard of the Highway Code though, so lots of jostling cars, mopeds and pedestrians all vying for road space. There are street vendors everywhere, little shacks selling roasted corn cobs and goat meat fritters, and stalls selling everything from pots and pans, clothes pegs and towels, to engine parts and tyres. There was a man selling outboard motors from the flatbed of a truck, another with huge vats of dark liquid that he was decanting into bring-your-own bottles, and an old man in a three-piece suit and bowler hat giving cut-throat razor shaves on the pavement. He must be good, and safe, as he had quite a queue forming.

When we got back to the Lodge, the children streamed off the minibus and I thanked Dann for including me and said I could now tick visiting Victoria Falls off my bucket list. He said he hoped one day I would be able to come back and see it in the dry season. Although you don't get the same awesome sight and sounds of the massive waterfall as we did today (interesting fact, he said over 600 million litres go over the edge every minute at this time of the year!), he thinks it is as impressive, just in a different way, as you are able to see the rock formations and striations, and the sheer scale of the ravine. He did have the good grace to add that perhaps that only appeals to him because he is a geologist! I said I very much hoped I would come back one day to see it again, and he said, 'That's a date then,' but then looked a bit embarrassed so excused himself, saying he'd remembered that he hadn't done a head count when the children got back on the bus so he wanted to check he hadn't left anyone behind.

Love

Anna x

Email from Izzy to Anna

Was that a 'moment'?

Email from Anna to Izzy

With Dann?

Email from Izzy to Anna

Yes.

Email from Anna to Izzy

No, I think it was just a turn of phrase, I don't think he meant date date. I'm sure he just likes to share his passion for his subject with everyone who goes to see the Falls and that he wants to encourage them back. The children's excitement and wonder is really infectious, particularly as most of them have never seen them before even though they are right on their doorstep. Dann's knowledge also helped bring the whole experience to life.

I just can't put into words what a wonderful day I had. Such an amazing place, and to share that experience with the children and Dann, of course, made it even more magical.

Love

Anna xx

Email from Izzy to Anna

It sounds amazing. I told Belle and she burst into tears! She seems so grown up most of the time that I sometimes forget she is just a little girl. She said she wished she was in Zambia with you and that she misses you. So, we had a nice mum and daughter afternoon out with a movie and pizza, which was a real treat for us both. I promised her that I am sure one day she will be able to see the Falls for herself, and that it's only a few short weeks until you are back with us.

Love

Izzy xx

✢

Email from Anna to Izzy

Hey big sis

Hope you are all well.

Classes at Twalumba finished a bit earlier than normal today so, on my way back to the Lodge, I had some time to wander around the school and peek in at some of the classes. Ella and her classroom assistant Bethsheba were making butterflies out of coloured paper and pipe cleaners with the Tiny Tots so they asked me if I wanted to help. I had a lovely hour showing the littlest ones how to use scissors, somewhat unsuccessfully, and coloured paper and glitter. Little Henry was right, he once told me that there was a lot of glue everywhere by the time they had finished! Ella hung all the butterflies up around the room on strings so that they fluttered in the breeze from the open windows, which seemed to please the children. It was then time for their afternoon nap so I said my goodbyes and popped my head around the door of the IT room, but the older students all looked like they were concentrating hard so I didn't disturb them.

Dann was teaching a lesson to some of the middle year's children in one of the open-sided classrooms. He had a blackboard and had drawn a cut-away picture of a volcano on it with coloured chalk and was explaining about the formation of magma. Oh, and I didn't know, but he wears glasses when he is teaching – he looked very academic. I think he saw me as he nodded in my direction but didn't stop talking and so I watched him for about five minutes and then walked home.

Love

Anna xx

Email from Izzy to Anna

Hi back

I expect you enjoyed making those butterflies, you always were the creative one in the family. Tom and I are both hopeless, so I know Belle loves it when you come down to visit – she is certainly a chip off your block, not mine! Honestly, give that girl a huge box of felt tip pens at Christmas and you don't hear a peep out of her until Easter.

Hmmm, glasses? Not surprised you mentioned them, I know you were always more into the slightly nerdy and studious Clark Kent look (but still hot!) than the over-confident, coiffured Superman type!

If I'm not very much mistaken, once again, sounds like Dann vs. Matt?????

Love

Izzy x

Email from Anna to Izzy

You're worse than Grace. I keep telling you, he is just a friend – actually, now less like a friend, more like an acquaintance.

Email from Izzy to Anna

And yet, you mention him surprisingly often?

Email from Anna to Izzy

Do I? I'm sure I write and tell you about everyone else here too.

Email from Izzy to Anna

Do you? I imagine the school has lots of teachers yet I don't think you've mentioned them once. From the way you write, you would think Dann is the only one there! Don't you think that's a bit curious?

Email from Anna to Izzy

Not really. Perhaps I do mention him a bit more because I know him better than the others, but he is just one of many colleagues at the school. If it makes you feel better, I can tell you Miss Amelia Banda teaches English and social sciences. Mr Damilola Totsi is the head of science, Mr Augustus Chuma teaches maths and Mrs Evangeline Sussi teaches I.T. and computer studies.

Better?

Email from Izzy to Anna

Nice try, but you aren't fooling me one jot!

Email from Anna to Izzy

If you must know, I actually had a very interesting conversation with Mrs Sussi only last week. She's had a fascinating life. Her father was a leading activist in the local independence resistance movement and when she was little, her whole family of twelve had to go into hiding for a year because the authorities were looking to arrest him on a charge of subversion.

I know Mr Totsi is originally from a tiny village in the Northern Province called Nsunda and was orphaned at the age of ten so had to fund his own way through school and university working in a variety of jobs, including butcher's mate, tailor's apprentice, pot-washer and child actor on a popular Zambian soap opera (true!).

Oh, and Mr Chuma was christened Augustus after the Roman emperor!

So there!!!

Love Anna x

May

Hi

Greetings from wildest Africa. How are the Rockbeare Rabble?

We're just in that strange weather here between the wet season and the cold dry season, so it has been a bit difficult to predict lately. One day it's tipping down, the next dry but decidedly chilly (well, at least for Zambia that is, still more like a nice warm spring day in England!). I definitely think it's only us Brits who are obsessed with the weather. No one here gives it much notice. I'd never thought before that some places don't even have seasons like we know them. Here it's either wet or dry, that's it lol!

Everything is going along very smoothly now at the Centre, after a few initial hiccups and false starts. We've added a few more classes to our timetable at the request of the ladies and word has obviously spread, as the number of women regularly attending now must be about one hundred.

I wasn't sure, but my 'Principles of Art' class has gone down really well – last week I had over twenty women who all seemed keen to learn about proportion and perspective! I'll admit it's been a bit of a baptism of fire for me, I've had to try really hard to remember everything I've learned over the years, but it has been an enjoyable experience too.

Our two student helpers, Mathilde and Carolina, have been a great help and are proving a real asset. Mathilde reminds me of me at her age, she is extremely enthusiastic and just loves passing on her love of design. Carolina is perhaps a little more reserved but the younger women particularly seem to have really taken a shine to her and think she is very exotic. We have one young lady who comes to the Centre called Agueda who is originally from Guinea-Bissau so has been happily chatting away to Carolina in Portuguese.

Some of the women here are showing themselves to be remarkably talented and creative, and it's lovely seeing how a bit of encouragement is giving them the confidence they need. We had a fun session last week, each of us trying out batik dyeing for the first time. Let's just say, some of them were more successful than others (i.e. me!). Using the long-handled canting tool to draw the wax on to the fabric isn't as easy as it looks.

I've also made my first woven basket – I've attached a photo. Don't laugh, I know it isn't perfect. The top edge is definitely a bit wobbly, but I was secretly quite pleased with the result. Obviously it's not good enough to sell, so I am going to take it back to my cottage and use it as a waste paper basket, but I am pretty sure I can get much better with a bit more practice. I hope by the time I leave here I will have mastered making traditional Moses cribs and shopping baskets, which my ladies think will sell really well.

Love

Anna x

Email from Izzy to Anna

Hey Anna

It didn't look that bad, a bit of wonkiness just makes it look home-made, which is a good thing.

If you have room in your luggage when you come home, can I put in an order for one of those wicker shopping baskets? I am in Belle's bad books (again!) and need to earn some brownie points. You know how passionate she is about the environment? She told me I had to throw away all my plastic shopping bags and find something more 'sustainably sourced' to put my carrots and tins of beans in. I think she's also really annoyed at me for telling her she can't become a vegan until she's eighteen, but then Tom doesn't help by insisting on eating his Sunday morning bacon sandwich right under her nose.

Kids! (Young and not so young.)

Love

Izzy x

✻

Hey sis

I had a really magical day yesterday, so thought you might like to hear about it.

As it was Sunday there were no classes at Twalumba, and it is usually the quietest day of the week here anyway. There are still plenty of visitors to the Lodge, but I don't see them at my end of the property and Grace has kindly put up a 'Private' chain across the little path to my cottage so that no one will wander in on me unexpectedly. There is a skeleton staff for an hour or two while most of them are at church. It is a lovely colourful sight to see all the women from the Lodge, the school and the surrounding villages in their Sunday best walking down the track towards the main road to catch the bus into Livingstone. Grace gets Thomas to drive her in one of Samuel's old cars, usually the lovely blue Healey. She always wears one of her gorgeous African print dresses with a hat and gloves, however hot it is.

I was happily swinging on my daybed after breakfast watching a resident hoopoe that visits my tiny patch of grass most days and keeps it free from ants for me. I have named him (or her!) Hoop (not very imaginative I admit) and we often sit out there together for a few minutes before it flies back to its roost.

As I looked up, I saw Dann walking down the boardwalk carrying a cool box. He said he had come out of his cottage this morning to find it on his doorstep, with a note from Grace saying, 'It is such a beautiful morning, why don't you ask Lottie if she would like to go out onto the river?'

He had swung by Lottie's room but she had said she wanted to get her latest research notes in some sort of order while it was quiet, so would take a rain-check. So Dann wondered if I would like to go with him so that the food didn't go to waste. Grace had packed enough sandwiches, pastries, fruit and water to feed a whole boatload of sightseers, with a bottle of wine and some beer for good measure. I wonder if she thinks Dann and Lottie need fattening up or perhaps just a bit of a romantic nudge? As well as the mountain of food, Grace had also packed two pairs of binoculars and one of Samuel's bird spotting books. I jumped at the chance to go, even as second choice.

Izzy, being on the Zambezi is exhilarating and terrifying in equal measure. It is so beautiful but you always know there is danger not far away, which I suppose is what makes you feel so alive when you are on the water. It certainly isn't like being on a day cruise up the River Dart and, as Dorothy Gale would say, it definitely isn't Kansas. I am guessing of course – I've never been to Kansas but don't imagine it is anything like here!

It isn't the danger you can see that you have to be careful of, it is what lurks underneath. The hippos are dangerous but are quite easy to spot. They sit for long hours in family groups on tiny raised sand bars, with just their snouts and ears showing. Sometimes it is hard to tell them from the rocks, but they waggle their ears a lot, which gives them away. It can be alarming if you get the boat too close to them, as they silently slip back under the water like the periscope of a submarine, so you just move away as quietly (and quickly!) as possible. The crocodiles are also dangerous, of course, and you certainly wouldn't want to try your 'wild swimming' here. They are mostly active at night, although Piet did say he heard once of a Norwegian tourist who was dangling her hand over the side of a wildlife-spotting boat – although not at Baobab, I hasten to add! – and had it bitten off by a crocodile. Don't worry, Piet has very strict river safety protocols here: no leaning over the side and arms inside the boat at all times.

Even if the hippos and crocs don't get you, there are plenty of big fish that might. There are massive, aggressive bull sharks in the river that Piet says are much more dangerous than a Great White, huge Vundu catfish that could swallow a dog whole and, my favourite, the Mbenga or Goliath Tiger Fish, a ravenous predator up to five feet long with teeth like giant daggers!

Thankfully, we didn't see any on this trip and Dann and I were far too focussed on our bird spotting anyway to worry about anything menacing beneath us.

I know people come to Africa to see the 'big five' and the wildlife on the land is really spectacular, but I think it is the birds I have found most captivating here.

Dann said his knowledge of the birds was still a bit patchy, despite Samuel being an excellent teacher, so if he spotted one, he tried to keep it in view with his binoculars and describe it so I could look it up in the book. Something along the lines of 'about a foot long, very long tail, red bill, pale pink breast, white belly, about ten in a flock' equals the 'red-faced mousebird' etc.

As well as the flock of mousebirds (or should that be micebirds?), we saw impossibly pretty bee-eaters and lilac-breasted rollers with their multi-coloured plumage as well as ibis, herons and swifts. We were also lucky enough to see a beautiful pied kingfisher just sitting on the branch of a submerged tree by the river bank. Dann took the boat over as far as we could go in the reeds without scaring it away, and I had time to make some sketches. I think it would make a stunning design for a new fabric so I am going to share it with the ladies at Twalumba tomorrow and see what they think.

On the trip back, we saw a big troupe of baboons drinking from the river, giraffes and a herd of impala. Luckily, all the dangerous wildlife lives on the Zimbabwe side of the river so we don't have to worry too much about any perilous encounters at Baobab!

Love

Anna x

Email from Izzy to Anna

Hey

Sounds like you had a lovely time and nice that you could spend some time with Dann, even as the substitute. What do they say? 'Fortune favours the brave' or, as I like to think, 'fortune favours those who are available'. Was it just the water that was brooding and menacing?

If all the same with you, I think I will stick with the boat to Brixham or perhaps go as far as the ferry from Teignmouth to Shaldon if I'm feeling particularly adventurous.

Belle, on the other hand, was inspired by your letter. She is having to do an essay about an animal of her choice. I think most of her classmates are doing kittens and puppies (or similarly benign fluffy things), but she is going to write about the Goliath Tiger Fish as she liked the thought of a huge fish with massive pointy teeth! We googled it – you are right, it is truly terrifying.

Love

Izzy x

*

Email from Anna to Izzy

Hey

Just letting you know we had some real drama here yesterday. Sadly, not good drama – very bad drama.

Dann had gone out just before dusk with Harold and their friend Moses, who is the Senior Wildlife Protection Officer in Mosi-oa-Tunya National Park. The rhino he looks after are protected around the clock by armed guards but even when he's not on duty, Moses still likes to check up on them. He says they are as precious to him as his own children.

Henry had told me his dad also likes to go with Moses when he can to look for pieces of fallen timber, particularly bits of hard wood like African rosewood or teak. The trees themselves are protected but he sometimes finds a felled limb, which he's allowed to bring home for carving. Next time you're visiting me, I'll show you a drawing Henry did of the crib his father made for the twins – it's beautiful.

I didn't know until yesterday, but Dann sometimes goes with them on their bush walk. He enjoys their company and while Harold looks for wood, Dann looks for interesting rocks. I suspect they also enjoy a bit of men-only time as

Henry says he has sometimes seen his dad putting a cool bag of beer into the boot of his truck before he goes off, but don't tell Hester!

It was late afternoon when they parked up. Dann said they had been walking for about fifteen minutes and had just passed the Old Drift Cemetery, where some early white settlers are buried, when they heard gun shots. Thank goodness, Moses always carries his rifle and radio, even when he is off duty, but Dann was only carrying his binoculars and a small rock hammer. Harold did have his old woodworking saw but nothing else to protect himself.

Moses was quickly on his radio to the other armed guards in the area but, like complete idiots if you ask me, they all just started to run towards the sound of the gun shots. I can't help thinking that running in the opposite direction may have been the more sensible option!

There was apparently a lot of confusion. Dann could hear the crackle of Moses's radio and the voices of the rangers who had been alerted by the gun shots and were running towards the commotion. As the three of them fanned out, Dann says that just by chance, he saw one of the would-be poachers stepping out from behind a tree on the edge of a mopane thicket.

I have no idea what possessed him, and I am not sure he does either, but he says he just ran full pelt towards the poacher, colliding with him with such force that they were both knocked to the ground.

The poacher had a high-powered hunting rifle but it apparently skitted away a few feet in the fall. Dann said he didn't stop to think, he just jumped on top of the poacher and they started to wrestle. He said the man was quite young, perhaps twenty years younger than him, and strong. Despite being winded in the fall and probably shocked, the poacher was fighting back hard. Dann says all he can remember was hitting the guy, and being struck in the face himself, and that he was just desperately trying to pin his arms down under the weight of his knees. He must have been shouting because thankfully Moses and Harold quickly appeared, probably within a minute, although Dann said it felt like an eternity. Moses grabbed the gun, which apparently was alarmingly close to the poacher's outstretched hand by that time, and Harold used his not-inconsiderable weight to sit on the poacher's legs to help Dann overpower him. He may have been younger, fitter and stronger but was probably no real match for the combination of Dann's military experience and Harold's size.

They managed to subdue him enough for Moses to call the park guards to their location on his radio, and they arrived about five minutes later to take him away. Dann said the poacher looked like the stuffing had been knocked out of him, but he still had a flinty defiance and cold, hard expression.

Another two poachers were quickly located hiding in some scrub and arrested by the other guards. The good news is that the rhinos were safe and completely unharmed. Thankfully, it seemed as if these poachers were pretty incompetent, not much better at running away than they were in the use of their rifles, but it's a constant battle for the guards, and next time the poachers may be cleverer and have luck on their side.

By the time Dann and Harold got back to the Lodge, they looked a sorry sight, battered and bruised. By total coincidence, Hester and I were just coming back from Twalumba and had taken a short cut through the parking lot and around the side of Reception when their truck pulled in. They were both filthy and dishevelled. Harold had ripped his trousers to shreds on some tangled thorn bushes and had scuffed his knees in the brawl. Dann had come off worst, though. He had a pretty deep cut on his cheek and a nasty bruise was already developing around his right eye, where the poacher had punched him. His arms and hands were also badly lacerated with thorn scratches and he had twisted his ankle in the fall.

As you can imagine, Hester and I were both livid that they had been so reckless and stupid to try to tackle dangerous and desperate armed men; they could easily have been killed. What if the poachers had been better trained or more determined? Did Dann think he could fight them off with his rock hammer? Given how lucrative it is, poachers are ruthless and will think nothing of killing guards as well as the rhinos if they have to. Moses said that sadly, many of his fellow rangers have been killed by poachers all over Africa while trying to protect rhinos and elephants. It doesn't bear thinking about.

I was really cross with Dann, but I think it was just the shock and thought of what could have happened. Harold didn't get off so lightly. Hester really shouted at him, although you could see the relief on her face. She said, 'You stupid old fool, what possessed you? You need to stay in your garden, you aren't built for tackling armed men!'

Esther got the first aid box and treated Dann's wounds with iodine and put a butterfly plaster on his cut. I told him it served him right that it stung so much. What was worse, despite the obvious danger, I think Dann and Harold had actually enjoyed the experience. Dann said he had forgotten how good it feels to get in a fight when you have right on your side, and he and Harold were smiling, but I think Hester's glare was sufficient to make them both have the good grace to look a bit sheepish.

Grace came over just as Esther had finished patching Dann up and has insisted he goes over to the emergency room first thing in the morning in case his cut needs proper stitching.

The national park guards will be popping by tomorrow as well to take a statement from each of them about the incident. It is useful intelligence gathering apparently and, in return for a more lenient sentence, the young poacher they caught has already given the authorities information about the wider rhino horn poaching operation across the border. The irony is that the poachers themselves only get a few kwacha for what they do – it is the big bosses up the chain who can make tens of thousands of dollars from each horn they harvest, so those are the people the guards really want to catch.

What a night!

Anna x

Email from Izzy to Anna

OMG, high drama indeed. They certainly had a lucky escape. Still, sounds quite exciting. You know us police officers, we love nothing more than a good punch-up with a criminal who's resisting arrest!

Izzy x

p.s. Did you feel a little bit turned on by Dann's bravery?

Email from Anna to Izzy

Absolutely not! He wasn't brave, he was stupid and irresponsible. I saw him briefly this morning – we passed on the boardwalk as I was going to Twalumba and he was off to the clinic. He'd just been to school and apparently all the children think he is some sort of superhero, so I said I hope they aren't going to encourage him to do anything as reckless again.

He is limping a bit on his twisted ankle, his eye is already an alarming shade of purple, blue, green and yellow, and the scratches on his arms and hands look really angry. But, as said, serves him right!

Anna x

Email from Izzy to Anna

Really, not even a little bit? I know Tom now sits behind a desk in a shirt and tie, but I never forget the time he was a rooky copper and arrested a prolific burglar after a two-mile foot chase and a tussle in the bushes. When he got home, he was dirty and dishevelled and looked damn sexy. I seem to remember that was the night Belle was conceived 😊

Izzy x

Email from Anna to Izzy

Too much information! Anyway, degrees of danger. I don't suppose Tom's burglar was equipped with a high velocity hunting rifle. I'm glad Tom did what he did that night though because we have our precious Belle to show for it, even if I don't need the detail lol.

Anna x

Email from Anna to Izzy

Hey sis

Just back from Twalumba so am planning a quiet evening in my lovely cottage and thought I would catch up with you.

I know it has only been a few short weeks, but I am just amazed at how easily I have adapted from the hustle and bustle of London to the peace and quiet here. I admit that for the first few days, I found the total darkness and utter stillness a bit disconcerting, but now I can't imagine the noise and light of home. Dusk is one of my favourite times. I love to take a cup of bush tea and a torch down to the edge of my little deck looking over the Zambezi and just watch the water as the light fades.

And then yesterday, while I was sitting quietly down by the water's edge, just idly watching Hoop pecking at the ants, thinking about my life, I thought I saw some tiny, almost imperceptible movement in the water, and when I turned my torch on, there were two bright eyes skimming the inky water, staring back at me! I've never been that close to a crocodile before, it couldn't have been more than ten feet away, but I trust Grace when she says the decking is built in such a way that there is no danger. We watched each other for a couple of minutes, for most of which I am pretty sure I didn't take a breath, and then it swam off so quietly it hardly made a ripple on the water. You certainly wouldn't see that on the Thames!

I hope all is well at home with you, Tom and the BFG?

I miss you all and I so wish you could be here with me to experience this utterly captivating place.

Love

Anna x

Email from Izzy to Anna

Hey

Lovely to hear from you.

All well here thanks. Tom is working late, some big case (hush hush stuff) so I'm just back from taking Freddie to tennis practice and Belle back to school for end-of-term play rehearsals, and I'm now making Georgia a costume for 'Dress as your favourite sea creature' day. Don't ask. You know I am rubbish at this sort of thing but let's just say a see-through dome umbrella and crepe paper streamers make quite a convincing jellyfish!

I confess I'm a bit jealous. It sounds perfectly lovely and peaceful where you are, unlike this mad-house, but should I be worried that you are 'thinking about your life'? Have you had some sort of epiphany or, worse, are you having an early mid-life crisis?

Izzy x

Email from Anna to Izzy

Hey

Don't worry, I am sure it is a passing phase, but there is

something so hypnotic and magical about this place. I can't put my finger on it yet, but the mixture of stillness and vibrancy is proving intoxicating and unsettling in equal measure. I thought I might miss the glamour of the London scene – after all, it's all I've known for years. All that travelling, all that socialising, all that worrying what to wear to make the right impression. Endless meetings in chic bistros, endless champagne in hipster wine bars. I know I should miss it but I just don't, and that's a bit scary.

You know me, all designer frocks and posh handbags, but since arriving I've been wearing nothing but shorts, vests and flip-flops, or the occasional cotton frock if I want to 'dress up'. Hair pulled back in a pony-tail and no make-up either, you would hardly recognise me. It is all very liberating. Just the thought of killer heels and pencil skirts has started to make me feel quite queasy.

Love

Anna x

Email from Izzy to Anna

Meant to ask, has Superhero 'Dann the Mann' fully recovered from his recent heroic escapade?

Izzy

Email from Anna to Izzy

Yes, pretty much healed thanks. His eye is still a fetching shade of yellow and green, and he will probably have a small scar on his cheek as a permanent reminder. He's been joking that he now has a damaged left leg and a damaged right ankle, so his limp has evened up. Thankfully, though, no more trips to the national park and no more encounters with armed poachers, nor for Harold. I don't think Hester will be letting him out of her sight for a long while to come.

The good news is that the information the young poacher Dann tackled gave to the local police was enough to round up the poaching gang ringleaders over the border. Turns out he wasn't quite as hard and cynical as he appeared. I'm not making excuses, but I think he was just poor and desperate. He'll probably serve a few months in jail but has told Moses that when he is released, he is going back to his home in Lesotho to work on the family farm. Although it is sad there will be others to fill his shoes, it's nice that at least one young man's days as a would-be poacher are well and truly over.

Love

Anna x

✽

Email from Anna to Izzy

Hey sis

Sorry I haven't written for a couple of weeks. It has been really busy here. Grace knows the retail zoning guy in Livingstone (another of her former pupils – who doesn't she know?!) so the ladies are hoping to get a weekly pitch at Victoria Falls Market from next week. We are working night and day to produce enough stock to sell and I am done in by the time

I get back after work. But I had to write and tell you about something that happened here recently. It has made me feel incredibly proud.

A young girl called Talu from one of the local villages started coming to Twalumba a few weeks ago. I am not sure how old she is, probably no more than eighteen, but she already has a baby boy called Precious and has another on the way. The ladies at Twalumba say she is supporting her husband Mazala as he was involved in a farming accident six months ago and lost a leg. Thomas lives in the same village and says Mazala used to be so active, but now just sits on the doorstep of their little block house all day as he cannot work. He waits from morning to evening for Talu to come back from her job as a cleaner at the airport, but when the new baby comes, they will be without any income at all.

The ladies say they think Talu is mute, as no one has ever heard her speak, but I thought she just seemed painfully shy. Every day when she didn't have a shift, Talu would come to Twalumba for an hour or so and seemed content to sit to one side on her own, working on some small sewing project or another. Thelma had heard she likes to sketch but no one has ever seen anything she has drawn or knows if that is true.

So, every day she was here, I made a point of sitting down and speaking to her and showing her some of my sketches. I talked to her about how I loved art and the craft of designing. She never replied although she did sometimes smile. About two weeks ago, I gave her a new drawing pad and a box of coloured pencils and said they were for her to take home as I had heard she liked to draw.

We didn't see Talu for a few days and then, last week, I

was sitting at the cutting table with some of the Twalumba ladies marking out dress patterns when Talu appeared at the door, Precious strapped on her back as always and the drawing pad in her hands.

She just came straight up to the table and said, 'Miss Anna, would you like to see some of my drawings?' Well, to say Thelma, Agnes and Delores were shocked speechless would be an understatement, and no mean feat as they love to gossip and chatter all day.

I took the pad from Talu and every page had a single exquisitely detailed colour pencil drawing of a Zambezi bird or insect or snake or spider on it. Honestly, Izzy, they were the most beautiful drawings I have ever seen.

Anyway, to cut a long story short, Grace thinks they will sell really well in the Lodge shop so she will buy as many drawings as Talu can produce and give her a generous percentage of every sale too.

Even better, Grace found out about Mazala and has employed him to be the Arts Centre custodian, with the wholehearted agreement of the Twalumba Ladies. He's in charge of stock, keeping the Centre tidy, repairing the sewing machines and stuff like that. Grace acquired an old wheelchair from the local hospital which Dann has fixed up (he repairs all the children's bicycles and said it wasn't much different) and Thomas now brings Mazala and his chair in every morning in the back of the Lodge van. He's getting used to wheeling it about and can now move quite fast over the polished concrete floor. He's already proving himself to be a great asset and, even better, turns out he is also a fine carpenter, so he is going to make the frames for Talu's drawings out of reclaimed wood.

Every day that goes by I feel myself connected to this place more than ever. I love the fact that Talu can now use her wonderful undiscovered talent to help support her family, and that Grace is a true African at heart and will always do whatever she can to help her people. I think it is that sense of selflessness that is so humbling. If someone here was hungry and all they had was a piece of fruit or a loaf of bread, you know they would still give half to their neighbour.

Anyway, hope everything good at home, write soon.

Love Anna x

p.s. Did Belle get her birthday card and present? It is quite hard to judge how long the post takes to travel from here to England, so I hope I gave it enough time. Does she like the bag? I bought it off one of the ladies at Twalumba called Inonge who made it especially for her, and was very happy because it was the first thing she has ever made that she sold. Tell Belle that Inonge is going to spend the money on a new school uniform for her son Kolo.

Email from Belle Rowbottom to Anna

Hello Auntie Anna

Thank you for my birthday present. I love it. It is a perfect size for my school books and Sophie, Evie and Jade are really jealous. Mum says I am the only girl in school with a one-off designer school bag made in Africa especially for me.

Can you thank Inonge for making it and let her know how much it has been admired? Do you think you could ask her to make me a matching pencil case? I have some pocket money saved up so would be happy to send this to you to give to her.

I miss you and wish I was there with you in Zambia. Mum lets me read most of your emails, it sounds magic.

Love

Belle xxxxxx

❖

Email from Anna to Izzy

Hey sis

Hope all well with you there.

I am starting to settle into a routine. I think the rain is getting a little less heavy and less frequent and there are definitely breaks appearing in the cloud cover. Grace knows the seasons here so well, she says she thinks it won't be long before it starts to dry up and gets a little cooler too.

Tomorrow is Saturday, and Grace has asked if I would like to visit Musanga Island. There's forecast to be a break in the clouds in the evening, so Piet is going over to give a talk about the stars to the couples who are staying there. As well as being so knowledgeable about the birds and animals along the Zambezi, Piet is also a very accomplished astronomer and Grace says his talks are one of the highlights for her visitors to Musanga, particularly as he weaves in a lot of very interesting local folklore.

Apparently, there are only going to be six visitors on the island tomorrow: a young French couple who are on their honeymoon, an American doctor and his wife, and an elderly Dutch couple called Mr and Mrs Rutgers. Grace says that unlike most of the visitors she has from the Netherlands, who speak excellent English, Mr and Mrs Rutgers only speak a little and she is worried they might miss out on their experience, so she has asked Dann to join us so that he can act as translator. It's the weekend so he isn't needed at school and Grace says she is sure her visitors would also be fascinated to hear more about the local geology and geography, especially of our part of the river.

As there are only three couples and six cabins, Grace has said Piet, Dann and I can all stay the night too in the three vacant cabins (the permanent staff have their own separate accommodation on the far side of the island). Piet says it is far too dangerous to be on the water after it is fully dark as that is when the crocodiles are most active, so we will return to Baobab in the morning.

I am really looking forward to it. It has been so cloudy recently that I haven't seen a proper African night sky yet, but I am told by everyone here that it is truly spectacular. Fingers crossed for tomorrow!

I will write again when I am back home.

Love

Anna x

✻

Email from Anna to Izzy

Hey

I've just got back from Musanga.

Izzy, I can honestly say it was one of the most truly magical experiences of my life. Piet was right, the rain did clear and the sky was such an inky black it hurt my eyes to look at it, like being down a cave or in a mineshaft.

First, the island. It is as lovely as I've been told. The cabins and buildings have been built with lots of local timber so they blend into the landscape. There is a small covered restaurant and lounge area, with comfy chairs and a library of books on Zambian wildlife. There is also a small bar and fridge for snacks, but apart from that, it really does feel as if it is off the grid. I know there is a basic bush kitchen and generator on the island as well, although both are well hidden behind some really strong fencing. It doesn't happen very often, but Piet says that in the dry season, when the river is particularly low, they have had the occasional herd of elephants wander over to the island to investigate, so they have to make sure all the supplies are secured away.

The island manager, Verity, had set up loungers around the central fire pit for us and the guests who are staying on Musanga. Amie and Alexander are on their honeymoon from Paris but seemed a little more interested in themselves than engaging with us, which is fine as they looked very much in love. Dr Hank Adams and his lovely wife May from Delaware were delightful, though, and seemed genuinely interested in talking to Dann about rock formations even though he apologised and said he hoped it wasn't a boring subject for such a beautiful evening. Grace was right, Mr and Mrs Rutgers did speak little English, so it was lovely to see their faces light up when Dann translated what Piet was saying. Grace is a very shrewd businesswoman – she knows that making her visitors feel welcome and special means they come back year after year, and then often become sponsors at the school too.

If I live to be a hundred, I don't think I will ever see anything as breathtaking as the African night sky. I've never actually seen the spiral arms of the Milky Way, created by billions of stars, before (who in England has?) and how they sweep upwards and outwards into the darkness. Piet says early Africans told many stories to explain the Milky Way, like how a young girl threw the ashes from her campfire high up into the night sky to guide her father home from a hunting trip. My favourite is that the milky curve of whiteness is actually the bellies of a vast herd of celestial waterbuck – isn't that enchanting!

It made me feel small and insignificant and actually quite moved. Piet says that is not a surprising reaction, and one he has heard many times from people when they see a proper African sky for the first time.

Oh, sorry, got to go. Someone's at my door. I'll pick up this email again later.

Love

Anna x

Email from Anna to Izzy

Hey

Me again!

Sorry about earlier, Esther was at the door. She had just come back from the market and bought some chikenduza buns that she thought I might like to try. They're like yeasty muffins topped with pink icing so I think I might find them a bit sweet, but it was kind of her to think of me. They went straight into my little fridge as the icing was already starting to melt.

Back to Musanga Island. I was in a cabin on the opposite side of the island, so facing away from the Zimbabwe bank across the river. That's where the best two cabins are. Grace said these are the most sought after as you can sit in bed or on your private deck and watch all the animals, like elephants and giraffes, come down to the Zambezi to drink. I think Dr and Mrs Adams were in number one, and the Dutch couple in the other. I think the French honeymooners were on my side of the island, but I don't imagine they minded the extra privacy.

So that no one misses out on their wildlife watching, the island also has a raised platform called the Observation Point in the reeds at the edge of the bank on the Zimbabwe-facing side with two sofas and a low table.

About 5 o'clock, I was just stirring. The sky was still dark but I think there was a small chink of light on the horizon as the sun was starting to rise. It was then I heard a quiet knock at the door. It was Dann. He looked a bit dishevelled, as if he had only just woken up, but he whispered, 'Quickly, do you want to see something amazing?'

I pulled on my sweater and shorts (don't worry, Dann turned his back) and put on my flip-flops and followed him outside, past the cold firepit and through the thorn trees to the Observation Point.

The air was so still and quiet but in the distance, I thought I could hear a strange rumbling sound. I must have looked a bit quizzical, but Dann just held up his finger to his lips. It was then that the sound started to get louder and closer, and it was beginning to resonate deep in my chest. Out of the gloom on the opposite bank of the river, I saw a herd of what must have been two hundred water buffalo, all running down to the water's edge. The sound of their snorting and bellowing was getting louder and louder, and great plumes of dust were being kicked up by hundreds of hooves on the hard soil.

They were so close you could almost touch them. I honestly don't think I took a breath for two minutes. When I looked at Dann, he seemed to be as mesmerised as I was and he was smiling (he has such a beautiful smile, it's a shame I haven't seen much of it). After about ten minutes, the water buffalo seemed to melt back into the gloom as if they had never existed, like some of Piet's ethereal spirit animals, and the spell was broken.

Apart from that magical experience and the night sky, there is so much more I want to tell you – like how the cabin I was in was open to the elements, which took some getting used to, particularly as Africa at night is full of wonderful and strange sounds; how an orange bird flew in this morning as I was packing my bag and just sat on my dressing table, pecking at its own image in the mirror; and why I think I am falling in love with Dann Huismann.

Love Anna x

Email from Izzy to Anna

OMG!!!!!

Email from Anna to Izzy

I know, right? I described it to Piet and he said it sounded like a white browed robin chat. He said they are fiercely territorial so will try to see off any rival, even when that rival is just their own reflection. They must get very confused when the other bird seems to be just as determined as they are!

Email from Izzy to Anna

Not OMG the robin chat (although it does sound charming), I meant OMG Dann!!

Email from Anna to Izzy

I know what you meant. 😊 Don't get overexcited. I said I think I am falling in love with him. There is absolutely no sign that he is doing the same with me.

Email from Izzy to Anna

Are you sure it isn't just a combination of too much African sun and good old-fashioned lust? Like the African sun, he is hot, after all!

Email from Anna to Izzy

Don't you think I haven't lain awake for nights now thinking about that?

It definitely isn't just lust. Granted, he is attractive, but there is also something deep and genuine about him. Matt was far more handsome – like a movie-star, people used to tell me – but Dann has an inner strength and kindness that I find so appealing. It is so hard to explain when I try and find the words.

I love that he is gentle and caring, but you also know he is fearless and loyal. He loves the things in life you should love, real things, important things, not artificial things like Matt.

Honestly Izzy, when I see him, everything speeds up and slows down at the same time, does that make sense?

Email from Izzy to Anna

Wow, you have got it bad, haven't you? Joking aside, sis, be careful. I don't want to see you hurt again x

Email from Anna to Izzy

Thanks, I know you're right as always... but I've got a horrible feeling it's already too late.
Anna x

June

Hey

It has been unseasonably warm here for a couple of days but I am really starting to get used to it. When it shines the sun is fierce, whatever the time of year, so I am staying in the shade as much as possible, and you do get a lovely breeze off the river.

The Twalumba Ladies had gone home a bit early today because of the heat. It can get quite warm in the Centre with all the machines on, so most of them are starting a bit earlier and leaving a bit earlier each day. Carolina and Mathilde have become firm friends and had today off to visit the Falls together.

I was sitting outside in the shade of the eaves with a big box of beads and some wire, idly making up some bracelets, when Grace joined me. I had forgotten how a simple creative task can give me such pleasure.

Grace had been out inspecting various parts of the Lodge

grounds with her site manager Willem and was a bit hot and tired, so I made us some tea and she sat with me for a while, stringing beads. She says she actually finds it quite restful and keeping her fingers agile helps with her arthritis. She said 'Anna, there is nothing to recommend old age' and I know she's right.

As we sat and worked, mostly in companionable silence, Dann and Lottie walked by and started down the long path to his cottage, which skirts around the Centre. They didn't look our way as their heads were very close and they seemed deep in conversation.

Grace looked up and said, 'Those two make such a lovely-looking couple. When they come along, and I pray they do, their babies will be beautiful and clever.'

I didn't trust myself to say anything, just grunted a little 'hmm' of agreement and then proceeded to search intently for a particular imaginary bead in the box in front of me as if my life depended on it and as if it didn't feel as if I had been hit in the solar plexus. When I allowed myself to lift my eyes a little, Dann and Lottie had rounded the corner towards his cottage and had disappeared from view.

I can't blame Grace for saying it, she doesn't know how I feel and she is right, of course, their children would be gorgeous. But I can't help but feel utterly miserable at the thought.

Izzy, I am not sure I can stay here much longer. I know I am good at putting on a front but every day I see Dann and Lottie together, my limited acting skills get stretched a bit more.

Love

Anna x

Hey

I seem to remember you were quite a good actress at school – you certainly had the lead in more school plays than anyone else. For a fifteen-year-old, didn't Miss Moon say your Norma Desmond was a tour-de-force?

And what about your Jane Eyre? Wasn't she thwarted in love by a brooding heartthrob she couldn't have? Although, having said that, don't get your hopes up that you'll eventually get your Mr Rochester and live happily ever after.

Don't they say that acting is behaving truthfully under imaginary circumstances? You just need to flip that and work on the grounds that 'acting is behaving untruthfully under real circumstances' instead!

Love

Izzy xx

Email from Anna to Izzy

Hey

Very funny but seriously Iz, what am I going to do? Just by his spectacular disinterest, Dann has made it clear that he doesn't want any sort of serious friendship with me, let alone a relationship, so what's wrong with me? I really think I am too old to be having these feelings of misplaced infatuation.

But even though I keep telling myself that, why can't I stop my heart pounding and that awful, sick feeling in the pit of my stomach when I am near him?

Love

Anna x

Email from Izzy to Anna

Don't like the sound of those symptoms. Perhaps you've got dengue fever?!

I know you think I make a joke of everything but, serious big sister tone for a mo, why don't you just tell him, Anna?

What's the worst that could happen?

Email from Anna to Izzy

Tell him! Definitely not!

Remember what I said when Matt left me? Quivering jelly on the inside, cold hard face on the outside. I've had enough humiliation at the hands of a man recently to take the risk again. I'm certainly not going to declare my feelings for someone who clearly doesn't feel the same and, in truth, is interested in someone else.

If I told Dann I liked him (loved him?), I would *literally* die of embarrassment, and I mean *literally* literally!!

I've still got to live here and see Dann nearly every day, so much safer he thinks I am as indifferent to him as he is to me.

Anna x

❖

Email from Anna to Izzy

Hey there

I think I have just been through the worst night of my life.

There has been a fire at Twalumba, and nearly everything has been destroyed. I was having a fitful night sleeping and at about 4 o'clock I thought I could hear shouting and screaming a little way in the distance. When I looked outside, I could see a huge column of black smoke rising behind the trees over to the left of the Lodge, somewhere behind the school.

By the time I had dressed and raced over there, I could see the building was well on fire. Dann, Harold, Piet and Thomas were already there, as was Grace in her dressing gown and a few of the guests from the Lodge who had been woken by the commotion, but there was little they could do. The men had formed a chain from the building, and Dann had been in a few times until the flames and smoke drove him back. It looked like he had managed to salvage a few sewing machines and some bolts of fabric, but very little else. Grace looked ashen. She said she had already called the fire department in Livingstone and they were on their way, but it would be at least twenty minutes before they could get there. The bad news is the Centre is far too far away from the river for anyone to carry any significant water up in buckets. If there is any good news, which I am not sure there is, at least the Centre isn't near any other buildings like the staff quarters or the school, and has few trees around, so the fire looked fairly self-contained.

Harold told everyone to get back, as pieces of burning cloth and paper were raining down. One piece landed on my arm and I have a small burn, but I didn't even notice. We all felt so helpless.

As we watched, a few more staff came up, and some more guests, and word had obviously spread as some of the

Twalumba ladies had arrived from the village. Joyce and Patience were there, holding each other and just staring in disbelief. Many of the women were crying, I think they knew that everything they had worked towards over the last few months – their fabrics, their designs, their equipment – was ruined. And it's not just the material things – I am sure over time they can be replaced – it's the fact that many of the local women have come to rely on this place, not just for their livelihoods but for companionship as well.

I just stood staring at the flames without moving, I think I was in such a state of shock. Dann saw me and came over, he was filthy with smoke and ash but he didn't seem hurt, thank God. He said, 'Are you okay?' and I just burst into tears. I don't think I have ever cried like that before in my life. Dann gently pulled me to him and just held me while I sobbed and sobbed into his shirt. I don't know how long for, could have been a minute, could have been ten, I just got to a point where there were no more tears and I was dry sobbing. At some point, Dann stepped back and gave me a tissue to dry my face. He looked grim but he didn't seem to mind that his shirt was soaked and snotty and I must have looked a complete state. I know my eyes were red and my throat hurt from crying.

We just all stared at each other; we had no idea what to do. Thankfully, the Livingstone Fire Department tender eventually turned up and we were all told to move away from the fire. To be honest, by then, it was starting to die down a bit as it had consumed everything that was flammable and the damage had already been done. Grace chivvied her guests back to their accommodation and then said she'd organise coffee and sandwiches for the rest of us back at the Lodge, so a few of us just walked back down the path like a group of zombies, not speaking and completely shattered by what had happened.

Grace asked Sarah to get the best brandy out, which she said was good for shock, and it did help.

This is a total disaster. I'm so numb, I don't know what to think or do next.

Anna x

Email from Izzy to Anna

Oh Anna, I am so sorry for you all. You've worked so hard over these last few weeks, no wonder you are all devasted. I feel helpless here but let me know if I can do anything to help.

Love
Izzy 😞

＊

Email from Anna to Izzy

Hi

We have all been back up to Twalumba this morning to look at the damage from the fire. Sadly, in the morning light, it is even worse than we had expected. The shell of the building is still intact, but all the timbers have burned away and the roof has collapsed in. There is nothing left inside. No equipment, no shelves, no fabric, no tables, no chairs. All the ladies' designs and half-completed work have gone, which is probably the most heartbreaking thing of all. Wet soot has run down the blocks and stained the ground black, and there is still a heavy, acrid smell in the air.

But despite the inevitable sadness, there is optimism this morning. Izzy, I don't know what to say but I truly love the people here. They often have so little and sometimes terrible things happen to them like this, but they are endlessly resilient and positive. No wailing, no self-pity, they just get up and start over.

Grace has been absolutely marvellous and heroic this morning, doing what she calls 'mobilising the troops'. She has already been up to the site with Esther to take photographs of the wrecked building to put on the Lodge website to start the rebuilding project fundraising drive. She has told George and Thomas to move Samuel's vintage cars out of their private garage. She says they will be just as happy living under the car port area by reception for a few months and we can use the space as a temporary workshop until the Centre is rebuilt.

She knows literally everyone in Livingstone and has spent the morning on the phone. First to Chief Fire Captain Musonda, who will come out this afternoon to do a report for the insurance claim, next her old friend Fusani, who was one of the original pupils at Mwabonwa and who now owns a second-hand furniture shop in town called 'Thrifty Interiors'. He says he has several worktables and assorted chairs we can have as well as some shelving units. No cost, he says, he just wants to do his bit to help. He told Grace that none of them match, but she said she wasn't starting a beauty parade, practical and functional would do just fine. Dann was able to save about six sewing machines last night, which will have to do for now, and Grace has asked us to take the van to 'Sew and Sew Fabrics' in town and load it up with as many metres, bales or bolts of assorted cloth as we can carry, as well as all the other bits and bobs we will need like cotton and needles. She said just ask Mrs Kawonde, the proprietor, to add it to her account.

The Twalumba ladies arrived during the morning from all over the district, some on bicycles but mostly on foot, many walking several miles to get here as they do most days. Joyce's husband owns a small bakery so, mid-morning, she and Patience arrived in the back of his bread van. Grace's garage is actually quite spacious with the cars removed, but we will need to do some serious tidying and cleaning, and perhaps spruce it up with a lick of paint before we can set up the furniture, which Fusani says he is happy to deliver by Saturday latest, and then reopen for business.

So, all hands to the pumps. I'll email again when we've made some progress.

Love

Anna xx

Email from Izzy to Anna

Great news to hear that everyone is determined to get back into business as quickly as possible.

I will check out the website later today to see if there is anything we can do here in terms of fundraising.

Your big sis

Izzy xx

❖

Email from Izzy to Anna

Hey

I was telling the Chief yesterday morning about the fire at Twalumba and he said, right off the cuff, would it help if we did some fundraising here? We were just about to have our regular Monday morning COs catch-up meeting so he added it onto the agenda and, great news, everyone has agreed that the Chief Officers' Landing should pitch in.

So, as of 11.30am, Team 'Run for Twalumba' has been created! We have decided on a 10k run across Dartmoor. We haven't figured out the route yet but will probably start and end at Princetown (we thought it would be fitting to have the prison in there somewhere).

So far, our team is all the top team and a handful of our lovely PAs, plus me and Tom (he is almost a CO and only just across the hallway so we thought that was ok). It has sparked a lot of interest across the force. Coppers are a competitive and sometimes ambitious lot, especially when it comes to (a) running prowess and (b) being in with the top team, so we might open it up to all officers who want to take part. The more people we have running, the more money we can raise.

I've printed off some sponsorship forms and have already taken mine down to A Shift, and Tom has handed his around some of the other departments he has worked in over the years. I think Mum and Dad are currently in Japan, but I've added them in for £100, I'm sure they won't mind. We've set ourselves a target of £2,000 but I reckon we could get well over that if we try hard enough.

I had Grace Nkomo's email from something you forwarded on, so hope you don't mind but I have dropped her a line direct to let her know.

Chin up!

Love

Izzy x

Email from Grace to Izzy

Dear Mrs Rowbottom

Many thanks for your earlier email, and for your very generous offer to fundraise for us here at Twalumba. It sounds like you have set yourself an epic challenge so I hope when the day comes your legs won't be too tired and the weather will be kind.

We will be thrilled with any amount of money you can raise for us. There is so much we need to buy, so I know it will go to very good use.

While writing, please let me say how much we truly love and value your sister Anna. Her support to the ladies here at Twalumba has been wonderful, and they have learned so many new skills under her expert tutelage. We all think of her as one of our Zambian family, and we are very proud of her, as I am sure you are.

With kindest and warmest regards, and heartfelt thanks from me personally and on behalf of all the ladies of Twalumba.

Grace (Nkomo)

❖

Hey sis

It's been a hive of activity here since the fire but, fingers crossed, we are very close to being able to declare our temporary home in Grace's garage OPEN!

It is much smaller than the Centre, about a third of the size I think, but is a solid building with lots of electrical sockets and good lighting, and even a small sink and cupboard space at one end where we can put our kettle. Even better, there is a small separate toilet that Grace insisted Samuel have built so he wouldn't have to traipse into the house in his oily overalls.

Grace got George and Thomas to box up all the miscellaneous garage detritus that everyone accumulates over thirty years – old paint cans, car repair stuff, gardening tools, boxes of nails and screws etc – and put them in her garden shed and in any bit of empty storage space they could find at the school. When cleared, it was remarkably spacious and it only took us a couple of days to get it ready for when Fusani arrived with the furniture. He was right, it is all mismatched but totally functional, and was just perfect to fit the space.

We are leaving the double doors open, and the tiny side windows, to create a through-breeze and, all in all, I think we have done a pretty good job converting an old garage into a useable art space in such a short space of time.

Following his inspection, Grace has heard back from Chief Fire Captain Musonda, who thinks the likely cause of the fire was rodent damage to some of the wiring where the anti-rat caging hadn't been adequately secured. He has done a report that will go to the insurance company, so hopefully there will be money to start the rebuilding work soon.

I think I mentioned before, but Grace has also started an official fundraising drive for additional funds to make the Centre bigger and better than it ever was before. She has been impressed by how much the local community have embraced it and, if we can raise enough, we may even look to add some extra space and even better facilities.

I'm just back at my cottage after a full day cleaning, painting, sweeping and setting up. I'm pretty grimy, I've chipped three nails putting up the new trestle tables and I've got paint in my hair, but I don't mind. I think I am what you would call dog-tired but strangely contented.

Off for a long hot shower otherwise I might just close my eyes and fall asleep here in my filthy overalls.

I'll write again soon.

Love

Anna x

Email from Izzy to Anna

I'm not sure I've ever seen you with so much as a hair out of place, so the thought of a dishevelled and dirty Anna Peel takes some getting used to. And chipped nails!! Are you sure you don't need a doctor lol?!

Izzy x

Ha ha, very funny. I've come to the realisation that being perfect is too tiring and time-consuming, so I can't help thinking I prefer this new Anna, imperfect but happy.

Anna x

✜

Email from Anna to Izzy

Hi Izzy

Just touching base, how are things with you? I hope the BFG are okay and Tom is back from his trip.

I wanted to write as the strangest thing happened late yesterday afternoon, and I have hardly slept trying to process it. I know you will call it a 'moment', which it probably was, but seriously, not in a good way!

There'd been a massive thunderstorm brewing all day even though the weather is now generally dry and cooler, which is a welcome relief at night as the humidity has made it quite uncomfortable to sleep sometimes.

The sky was so dark and threatening, it felt like it was night-time at 4 o'clock, and the electricity in the air was cracking so much it made the hairs stand up on my arms and the back of my neck. Do you remember that time in Grandad's caravan when all three of us were terrified because of that massive storm, and Dad said the only good thing was that he couldn't hear us all wailing at a thousand decibels

213

over the noise of the rain beating down on the metal roof? Well, imagine that, but tenfold.

During one of the rainy lulls, I had gone up to the Lodge office for some more supplies as I find I have had a real liking for bush tea since I've got here and I was out of milk and teabags. I blame Alexander McCall Smith. Esther was there holding the post but looked a bit harassed. She was just about to start her rounds of the staff quarters but there was a problem with the receptionist's computer, which kept flashing on and off – static in the air, most likely. As I was already out and about I said I would be happy to drop the mail around.

I don't go to the staff quarters very often but I do know where most people live. Henry was still at school but there was a letter for his father, so I stayed for a short while playing with the twins while Hester finished making some vegetable stew for their evening meal. I then dropped a letter into Thomas. His mother is only in Livingstone but she doesn't have a computer and, as he only goes home once a month, she writes to him without fail every week. The last piece of post was a small parcel for Dann. It was postmarked 'Alkmaar, The Netherlands' so I presumed from his mum and dad. Perhaps it was some of that Dutch chocolate he likes but can't get here.

I haven't been to Dann's accommodation before, although I know where it is. All the other teachers live off site, but Samuel and Grace let Dann have his little cottage when he arrived five years ago and he has lived there ever since. It's detached, and very private, and he has a small garden at the front, which is mostly left to native bush but is quite pretty, fenced in and with a wooden gate.

There were a few of those big fat raindrops starting to fall but I thought I could let him have his letter without any delay and get back to my cottage without getting too wet. It really is like stair rods here when it starts to rain.

I knocked but, not surprisingly, there was no answer as school wasn't due to end for another ten minutes, so I just opened the door and went in. No one here locks their houses day or night.

I felt guilty being in his private space, not sure why. The main room was neat and quite austere, with a small kitchen to one side. Definitely no sign of a woman's touch but not unpleasant. I should have just left his letter on the side table, which I know is what Esther would have done, and I have no idea what possessed me but the door to his bedroom was ajar so I stepped inside for a look. Just being curious (nosey?), I am telling myself this morning. It was a small room with some traditional dark wood furniture and a neatly made bed. I wasn't surprised; I can't imagine an ex-military man with an unmade bed. I have no idea why but the sight of his bed made something in my chest rock a little.

There was a framed photograph on the bedside table that I could see from the doorway, which could only be his wife and son. I have no idea why but I went over and picked it up. It was a lovely natural pose. It looked like it had been taken on a beach. His wife was so pretty and the first thing that struck me was how like Lottie she looked. She had a short blond bob and a wide smile and she was holding her son on her hip. He looked about three or four, just as fair as her but with brown eyes.

I think I knew Dann was standing in the doorway behind me before I heard him. It just felt like all the air had been sucked out of the room.

In truth, I was rooted to the spot, like a burglar who has been caught with his hand in the safe. I just whispered, 'Your wife was very beautiful' (as if that was the most natural thing to say when you are caught in a man's bedroom uninvited) and composed myself enough to turn around. Dann was wet. I could hear the rain starting to beat on the roof and he was breathing quite fast, so I expect he had run all the way from school.

He came and stood so close to me that I thought we were going to touch, but he just took the photograph from my hand and said, 'Please don't come here again.' His tone was flat and I couldn't fully read his expression, but I could tell he was really angry. I don't blame him – I would be too if some stranger was in my bedroom poking around in my personal possessions.

There were three seconds that felt like an eternity and then I think the tension broke a bit. I mumbled something about coming around to bring his post, gave him his parcel and walked out with as much dignity as I could muster, although I have to confess my legs were shaking so much I wasn't sure I would make it outside in one piece. The rain was really torrential by that time so I got soaked getting back to my cottage at the far end of the property, which served me right.

You know, when we first started to write, I thought Dann and I did have a bit of a connection, but lately he has been really distant with me and I just don't know what has happened to cause this change. I wonder if Lottie is the quiet, jealous type and has warned him off having any sort of friendship with me? Whatever, I am sure my antics yesterday have done nothing to endear me to him.

What should I do? Given what he said, which was pretty

blunt, I think I favour staying out of his way as much as I can for the rest of my time here. How hard can that be?

Agreed?

Love Anna x

Hey

I know you are the beautiful, serious and clever one, and I am the mildly pretty, savvy and quirky one, but just imagine that your big sister knows best for a moment.

Rather than thinking he was angry, could he actually have just wanted to throw you on the bed and ravish you? Was that feeling of electricity nothing to do with the storm and everything to do with pent-up sexual energy?

Despite his A-Lister looks, Matt never struck me as the most exciting person in that department, if you know what I mean. I thought he was a bit of a cold fish so perhaps you aren't best placed to recognise what happened with Dann for what it was? And anyway, the thought of Matt having any 'sexual energy' makes me feel a bit bilious. Was it like going to bed with a shop mannequin?

Izzy x

Izzy

Get serious for a moment please. No, Dann was livid, I could see it in his eyes.

I love you, but you have been no help whatsoever. I think I am going to go with the avoidance tactic.

Anna x

✣

Email from Anna to Izzy

Hi sis

Sorry I haven't mailed for a few days. We've been so busy at the Centre, I've hardly had time to think. I had worried that the fire would have put the ladies off but, if anything, there are more of them coming every day than ever. We have had so much demand that Grace has erected two awnings, one on either side of the garage, for the ladies to work in when they don't need to use the sewing machines or other equipment. It is now quite cool so it is extremely pleasant to work outside, and although we are now bordering on cramped inside the garage, no one seems to mind.

The work that was destroyed in the fire – dress patterns, half-finished garments, draft designs, sewing projects, drawings, beadwork, baskets – is all being recreated with gusto and without any grumbling. A lady called Ada, who had spent hours working on a beautiful batik fabric, just said, 'Miss Anna, it wasn't very good, I am glad to be able to start again. This time it will be ten times better.'

I just can't tell you how inspiring, uplifting and utterly joyous I find working with these amazing women. One day last week, one or two of the ladies started to sing a traditional song of rejoicing and then everyone else started to join in. They pushed their worktables to one side of the room and started to dance. You would have been embarrassed but they dragged me in and encouraged me to dance with them. I wasn't very good but they didn't mind. It is utterly infectious when you start and I loved every minute of it.

We only stopped when Thomas and Dann put their heads around the door. They had been walking up the path on their way to the Centre to finish putting together some flat-pack shelving. Thomas said he could hear our singing on the other side of the school, and he soon joined in. He's a very good dancer too, who knew? When I looked up though, Dann had gone.

Love

Anna x

Email from Izzy to Anna

Hey sis

Perhaps he is trying to avoid you just as much as you're trying to avoid him? Anyway, how are those tactics working out for you?

Izzy

Email from Anna to Izzy

Hey back

Okay, mostly. For the first few days after what I'm calling

the 'unfortunate bedroom incident', I think we were both just determined to avoid each other. If we do see each other, we haven't been saying much, just a passing 'hello' or a nod. A bit awkward but thankfully we don't cross paths too often.

Then yesterday, I almost literally bumped into him near the shell of the old Arts Centre. Not sure why I went up there, I was just walking and lost in thought when he came around the corner from the football field and we nearly collided. He was limping so I asked him if he was alright. He said he was just back from practice and that he had overdone it a bit but was fine. Henry's under-12s team are off to play their semi-final of a local cup competition next week so he said they were keen to get in lots of extra training. He said, 'I am getting too old for this,' but he did smile, so I am hoping he has thawed a bit and we can pretend the bedroom thing never happened.

Pleasantries, selective amnesia and indifference are much safer ground for me to be on with Dann.

Love

Anna x

✻

Email from Anna to Izzy

Hey sis

I had such a sweet conversation with Henry earlier today.

The under-12s won their semi-final yesterday and have

reached the finals of the local cup competition that is run in the district. They will be playing a team from Harry Mwanga Nkumbula School for Boys in Choma next Saturday afternoon.

Of course, as you can imagine, all the boys are extremely excited about their cup appearance, although it will be a big ask to beat HMK as they have much better facilities at their school than we do at Mwabonwa.

Dann is apparently a master at the pre-match pep talk though. Henry said he told them that it doesn't matter who is favourite or if the other team are stronger, bigger, faster. He said the 'Mwabonwa Mambas' can win with a positive attitude, solidarity, discipline, communication and sticking to their game plan. I suspect rallying the troops is something Dann has had to do a million times before.

Anyway, back to Henry. He came to see me with Harold in tow. Apparently, many family members of the whole team are going to watch the match. They think they can tip the balance with lots of extra shouting and cheering. Dann has told them that it's sometimes called having a 'twelfth man'!

Unfortunately, Harold had planned to go to support Henry but won't be able to now as that's the day he has a commitment in town with an important horticultural importer, who's coming all the way down from Kitwe. He's been trying to meet up with him for months so can't reorganise the meeting at such short notice. Hester is looking after the babies, Mabel is at her Saturday job in the salon and Milimo is up to her eyes in revision so can't be spared.

So Henry said, 'Miss Anna, would you come along as my family supporter?'

Of course, I couldn't refuse such a sweet request. Next Saturday afternoon, me (as an honorary Sissonga), Mr Munyama and Mr Tembo, fifteen excitable under-12s and a whole cast of family and friends will be off to neutral ground at Livingstone Academy to cheer on our team. Of course, Dann will also be there, but there will be a lot of people around and he will be busy so I am sure we can manage to stay suitably distant for a few hours.

Wish us luck. I will (hopefully) write next week with a photo of the team holding the cup!

Love

Anna x

p.s. Good luck with your run on Monday.

✽

Email from Izzy to Anna

Hey sis

My fingers and my eyeballs are the only parts of my body that don't hurt today which is why I can email.

Yesterday was fun but so much harder than I thought it would be. Thankful for small mercies, there was a lovely cool drizzle that helped, but I hadn't realised how hard it is running on a moor. I like to think I'm quite fit but I think I've got a bit soft just pounding the village roads. Up on the moor it's all grassy hillocks and hidden divots. You have to concentrate so much on where you're putting your feet, it's really tiring. No wonder the air ambulance spend half their time up there picking up walkers with broken ankles!

Anyway, we stuck together for the first mile or so, but then some of the stronger runners, like the Chief and Tom, sprinted ahead and I was left behind. I had told Tom before we set off not to wait for me, but you'd think he could have ignored me. I want to say I at least beat the Chief's PA but, despite her normal twinset and pearls, it turns out she ran cross-country as a teenager so she was actually pretty good. Long story short, I finished in mid-table obscurity, but at least I finished, woo hoo!

Feeling it today though. My thigh muscles are so tight that when I knelt down to get the clothes out of the washing machine, I wasn't sure I was going to be able to get up again. Honestly, I thought I was going to have to stay on my knees all day until Tom got back from work. Annoyingly, he is as fresh as a daisy.

Anyway, aching muscles notwithstanding, we did a quick ready-reckoning before we set off and we've smashed our target – we think by the time we have all the money in, it will be well over £5,000.

Love Izzy xx

Email from Anna to Izzy

Hey

That's fantastic! I don't tell you often enough how amazing you are, but you really are. We'll be able to do so much with that money. I can't wait to tell Grace, she'll be thrilled too.

When Tom gets home, get him to give you a rub down with some liniment. Who knows what you and Tom find spices things up in the bedroom. Given your track record, perhaps it could lead to you conceiving baby number four lol!

Love

Anna xx

*

Email from Anna to Izzy

Hi

This email is in two parts. An 'Oh, that's great news' part and an 'OMG' part. You'll see what I mean when you've read it.

The 'Oh, that's great news' is WE WON! I am hoarse from shouting but do feel like a very proud parent, even if only as a surrogate one to Henry.

It has been seen as a great success at Mwabonwa and there have been lots of celebrations since we got back from the game. I know you can't stand football, so won't bore you with the details, but it was a nervous match with little to choose between the sides until the team's golden-boy striker and captain, Charles Chola, scored in the 89th minute. Even though he is only eleven, Charles has already been scouted by Green Buffaloes in Lusaka and everyone thinks he could easily play for Zambia one day. Dann looked so nervous through the whole match, pacing up and down and shouting directions. He is very sweet sometimes. He wanted this so badly for the children.

Photo attached. Henry is third from the left, Charles is deservedly in the centre holding the cup.

As you can imagine, there was a lot of screaming, jumping around and hugging along the touchline when Charles scored and a lot of very stressed parents until the final whistle blew.

I'd been pacing up and down towards the end of the match too. Do you remember what I was like when we used to go and watch Robbie play? I just get too nervous to stand still. Well, I found myself standing next to Dann when Charles scored, and he grabbed me and we hugged each other for a moment.

Now for the OMG part. We broke slightly apart as if we had just realised what we were doing and stared at each other. All the noise around me seemed to fade into the background and the people became blurred and slowed down, as if I was underwater. All I could see was Dann's face. He looked momentarily confused, as if he felt the same thing, and then he pulled me back to him and kissed me and I kissed him. I don't know how long we stood like that, but suddenly the cheering and noise returned, the spell was broken and Dann stepped away as Mr Munyama ran over to shake him firmly by the hand and pat him on the back, clearly oblivious to what had just happened.

I don't think anyone saw. I suspect not – there was a lot of hugging and jumping up and down with excitement so it probably just looked like a casual, meaningless embrace to anyone who was even bothering to look in our direction for that few seconds. But it wasn't casual or meaningless to me and now I have no idea what to do.

I'm now home. As soon as we got back to the Lodge, I made some excuse about having a headache and left the celebration party before it got into full swing. Dann's gaze followed me as I left but he didn't try to stop me so I kept my eyes down and just hurried away. I thought he might turn up at my door but he hasn't. If I pace up and down any longer I am going to wear a hole in my rug, so I'm just emailing you and then going to bed, although I suspect sleep will be eluding me tonight.

Love

Anna x

Email from Izzy to Anna

As soon as you and Dann have 'had the talk', email me, day or night. I'll be on tenterhooks until then.

Love

Izzy x

p.s. I know I shouldn't, but I *am* secretly enjoying this 'will they, won't they?' And can you blame me? Yesterday I caught Tom in the bathroom, dressed only in a grungy old Black Sabbath t-shirt – which, by the way, left absolutely nothing to the imagination – cutting his toenails over the toilet bowl! Even if this DAnna 'thing' ultimately comes to nothing, I'm not ashamed to say how much I'm enjoying it so far.

✻

Email from Anna to Izzy

Izzy

What am I going to do? I have never felt so humiliated in my life, and don't forget my husband left me for a younger and slimmer woman!

I've been in a low-level state of turmoil ever since Saturday. So many emotions running around in my head: excitement, hope, worry, fear. I've been trying to carry on as normal with work, but there was no sign of Dann on Saturday night or Sunday either, or Monday or Tuesday for that matter.

Well, now I know why. About an hour ago I was at home folding some clean washing, when there was a knock on my door. I thought it was Esther as she had said she might pop over as she had a couple of minor queries about the Twalumba accounts.

So I hadn't expected to see Dann there. He looked tense and he certainly wasn't smiling. Instinctively, I suppose, I said, 'Would you like to come in?' but he just stood rooted to the doorstep and said, 'No, this won't take long.'

He then proceeded to tell me that he was sorry for what had happened on Saturday afternoon, that he had been thinking about it for the last three days and had come to the only rational conclusion that it was just an unfortunate mistake brought on by the collective excitement and a moment of madness.

But then, to add insult to injury, he said, 'I think after what happened, it's obvious I find you very attractive, Anna, but there can never be anything serious between us, and if you just want a casual, physical relationship, I'm sorry but I'm not in the market for that. It's just not my style.'

I was shaking with so much anger and hurt inside that I didn't think I was going to be able to speak but thankfully I managed to channel more of the anger than the hurt. Dann must have seen how steely I suddenly looked, as he seemed momentarily puzzled, which at least gave me some satisfaction.

I stared at him with as much cool disdain as I could manage under the circumstances and said, 'I totally agree that it was a one-off and I would be happy if we never spoke of it again. But, as you obviously think I am the sort of woman who would jump into bed with any man available, you clearly don't know me at all. If you did, you would know it's not my style either, so your apology is meaningless and your arrogance is breathtaking. You've done nothing but insult me by coming here today and frankly, you've made it even more clear to me that you are the last man I would ever want to have a relationship with, physical or otherwise." At which point, I slammed the door in his face with as much force and confidence as I could muster, but not before I could see that he perhaps looked a little surprised.

I leant back on the door for a few minutes until my heart had at least stopped pounding so loudly in my chest I feared he might hear it. When I dared peek outside, he had gone.

There is absolutely no way I can stay here now. If there was ever any stupid, deluded doubt in my mind that I could make him have feelings for me through my sheer will, those have been blown away in an insulting, bitter exchange that took less than thirty seconds.

So, you may be enjoying the 'will they, won't they?' but I think I can definitely say now that they won't. 😖

Anna x

Email from Izzy to Anna

Ouch!

Well, I've never been grabbed and pashed by someone who didn't fancy me so at least he was honest enough to admit he is attracted to you. Not making excuses for him but, given that he kissed you, he must be conflicted over his relationship with Lottie too, so perhaps he was temporarily addled by confusion and wanted to do the right thing? Also, shows he has some decency as it would have been easy to just drag you to bed and think nothing more of it.

I love you but just perhaps you were a bit harsh? I did like your speech though, reminded me of when Elizabeth Bennet blows off Mr Darcy!

Sorry, shouldn't be flippant because I know you are really hurting over this. I am here for you whenever you need me, us big sisters have very broad shoulders to cry on and long arms to hug with, even over thousands of miles.

Write soon.

Love

Izzy xx

Email from Anna to Izzy

Do you know what the worst part is? If he had said he didn't want any sort of committed relationship with me, but *was* okay with casual, meaningless sex, I am not sure I would have said no. You know I've never been that sort of person, so the thought makes me feel cheap, but I am in love with him so I would gladly have taken whatever scraps from the table I was offered, if he'd offered them, which he didn't. 😫

I am so miserable.

Anna

Email from Izzy to Anna

Oh Anna

I know I've been teasing you about Dann but it actually breaks my heart to think you are hurting so much. I know you will back soon anyway – do you think you can hold on until then? If not, why don't you come home early? Flights can be changed and excuses can be made. The sooner you're back home with us, the sooner you can forget Zambia and Dann.
　　Love
　　Izzy xx

❖

Email from Anna to Izzy

Hi big sis

Sorry to be emailing so late, it is nearly 2am here so think it is just after midnight with you (unless the clocks have changed, I've lost track)?

　　Don't panic, I am fine, but I'm currently at Livingstone Central Hospital. I just needed to tell someone, as I am really scared.

　　Dann got admitted earlier today – he has malaria and isn't responding well to treatment.

　　I was just at the end of my section of boardwalk when I saw Esther hurrying in the other direction, talking fast into her walkie-talkie. She says it is her most useful piece of equipment for keeping track of all the staff on such a big property. She looked worried so I asked her what the matter was and she said Dann had collapsed in Reception.

When we got there, he was thankfully sitting on one of the big comfy chairs drinking a glass of water, but he didn't look well. Luckily, the man who delivers the bottled water was in Reception at the same time so was able to help him up. Dann was very pale and sweaty. I hadn't seen him for days but any lingering anger after what we said to each other was instantly overtaken by worry.

I couldn't stop myself reaching down to touch his forehead. It was clammy and cold but he said he was really hot. He thought then that he might have malaria – he said he had it once before when he was bitten by a mosquito on manoeuvres in Central America and hadn't reacted well then either. No one here takes anti-malaria drugs like the tourists do, it would be too expensive, so most people just try to avoid getting bitten and if they are unlucky enough to get malaria, they just get treated for it then.

Dann hasn't been so lucky. As soon as Grace saw him, she immediately called the doctor.

He's now in hospital and is being given anti-malaria medication intravenously but is floating in and out of consciousness and seems quite dazed and confused. Grace has kindly paid for him to have a small private side room at the hospital rather than be on the ward, so I've been sitting with him since four this afternoon. I've just come outside for a walk and to stretch my legs, so thought I would message you. My back is singing from sitting on a hard chair all day and my head is pounding.

Grace called earlier. She asked if I wanted anyone to come in and take over from me but I said no, I couldn't leave him and I was fine. She says Lottie gets back from her field trip to Mozambique in the early hours of tomorrow morning so they will both come over just after nine. She has told me not to worry, but how can I not?

The doctors have popped in to see Dann a few times, look at his notes and then leave without saying a word. I don't know whether that is a good thing or a bad thing.

There is a lovely staff nurse here called Kasonde, she has been bringing me cups of strong sweet tea and biscuits all day. She asked if I was his wife. I said, 'No, just a friend.' She said, 'You are a very good friend then,' and I wanted to cry.

He is usually so strong but he looks so helpless. Kasonde gave me a bowl of cold water and a flannel, and I've been cooling his face and arms. He is sweating such a lot. Kasonde says this is quite a common symptom. His eyes are closed now but I am not sure if he is asleep or awake. He keeps muttering but I can't understand what he is saying.

Izzy, what will I do if he dies? Hundreds of thousands of people do every year and I don't think I will be able to bear it, especially after all the angry words between us. I've never even had a chance to tell him that I love him.

Anna

Email from Izzy to Anna

Hey sis

Don't worry about the time, you know you can contact me whenever you need me, and Tom and I have just got in from a work do of his, so we are still up.

I am so sorry to hear about Dann, but you have to try to

be positive. I am sure he will be fine and he is in the best place.

And when he is well again, you must tell him!

I will say a prayer for you and Dann. Stay strong and keep me posted.

Love from us all here,

Izzy x

✣

Email from Anna to Izzy

Hey

Me again.

Good news, Dann is awake. He still looks pale and is very tired, but Kasonde says his temperature is well down and he has stopped sweating. I have never been so relieved about anything in my entire life.

But my heart is still broken. After I'd emailed you, I went back to sit at his bedside. I was holding his hand and babbling inanely about everything and nothing, about you and the children, the weather in England, school, silly family stories, and then he squeezed my hand. He didn't open his eyes but he just said, 'I love you.' I was elated, for about five seconds, and then he said… 'Lottie'.

My heart is a bit bruised right now but I am just relieved he is alright. If he loves Lottie, I can live with that, as long as he is going to be okay. That's all that matters. I just wish this crushing ache in my chest would go away. When Matt told me had found someone else and was leaving me, I felt sad, disappointed and betrayed, but never this pain.

I'm now back at the Lodge. Thomas drove Grace and Lottie over to the hospital at about 10 o'clock. When Lottie came in, she rushed over and gave Dann the biggest hug so I slipped away.

Grace and Lottie will sit with him for an hour or two, so Thomas brought me back and he will drive back over after lunch to collect them. I don't think I will go, there must be a lot Dann wants to say to Lottie, and her to him, and three is definitely a crowd.

Off for a hot shower and to try to get some sleep.

I'll email when I have more news.

Anna

(And thank you for being the best big sis, I love you.)

✽

Email from Anna to Izzy

Hey sis

I feel a lot better today – well, physically anyway. When I got back from the hospital yesterday, I had a hot shower and went straight to bed. I didn't fancy anything to eat though, I think I have lost my appetite.

I didn't think I would sleep but I expect all that nervous energy eventually caught up with me and I slept though from about midday until 6 o'clock. By the time I woke up, Grace and Lottie were back from the hospital. Grace said Dann is going to be discharged tomorrow morning, so she is going to make up the spare room in her private apartment in the Lodge so that he can recuperate for a few days in peace and quiet. She said she knows he is feeling better as he is back to his stubborn ways and is already talking about coming back to work. She said he asked after me, which was nice.

Speak soon.

Anna x

p.s. I know I am due home in three weeks anyway, but I think you are probably right. I may speak to Grace about leaving early if I can change my flight. It will break my heart even more to say goodbye to her, my ladies, Henry and Zambia, but I don't think I can be here now. I will make up some excuse about being needed back at work – not sure what but I am sure something will pop into my head.

Email from Izzy to Anna

Hey

Yes, come home. Don't go straight back to London though, come down to Rockbeare for a few weeks. The BFG would love to see you, it has been a while and they are growing up so fast, blink and you miss it. Yesterday, Georgia rode her bike without stabilisers for the first time, and Belle is so excited about going to big school in September that she is already nagging me to buy her new uniform and the summer holidays don't start for another month!

I'll banish Tom and the kids so we can have some girly nights in, make cocktails and talk about all the men we've loved and lost.

I'll get the spare room ready.

Izzy x

Email from Anna to Izzy

Hey

I've rebooked my flight so will be back in London on Thursday (it is breaking my heart to leave now that I know I am).

The wi-fi has been patchy here for a few days – weather conditions, I think – but Thomas was driving into Livingstone to pick up some supplies from the hardware store so I slipped away without anyone seeing so he could give me a lift to the airport. There was a very nice lady on the ticket desk there who said that, by luck, a seat had become available on the flight down to Johannesburg in two days, so I have taken it. Even better, she was able to reschedule my flight to London as well.

If the offer still stands, I would love to come down for a few days. Ellie wasn't expecting me back until the end of the month anyway, so she is fine to hold the fort until then. I'll double-check the train timetable when I get home but should be with you sometime on the 12th. Don't worry about picking me up, I'll get a taxi from Exeter. Can you leave the key in the usual place if you go out?

Still not sure what to tell Grace. I am a terrible liar. I hope she doesn't ask too many questions and I hope I don't cry.

Love A x

p.s. Tell the BFG that Auntie Anna will need a lot of hugs.

❖

Email from Anna to Izzy

Hey

Don't be mad but I told Grace that I was leaving in two days time because I am getting back with Matt. I was concocting some elaborate tale in my head about unexpected work commitments when I bumped into her outside Reception. I think I panicked and wasn't sure what to say, so just blurted it out. She looked a bit shocked for a moment but, to give her her due, she regained her composure quite quickly and then smiled and hugged me and said she was so glad for my happiness, which made me feel like even more of a fraud.

I have just been to tell Henry. He was at home, and he cried and clung to my leg and said, 'Please don't go Miss Anna, I love you,' which was even more heartbreaking. Hester was very kind – she said they would all miss me but hoped I would come back again soon. I said that was probably unlikely, but I promised Henry I would still write to him every week.

I am just starting my packing so will be ready to go first thing on Wednesday, and then I'm off to tell the Twalumba Ladies. The flight from Livingstone leaves at 9 o'clock so Thomas has said he will wait outside with the car at about seven.

I will email you when I am back at Jo'burg airport.

Love Anna x

p.s. No sign of Dann today.

Hey

I might have gone with 'There's an international crisis in hat-making and only I can save the millinery world' or something similar, but getting back with Matt is also plausible. I hope there isn't even a grain of truth in that – you know I will be cross if there is.

Safe journey. Let me know if there are any delays as I will worry about you until you are home.

Love

Izzy xx

❈

Hi

Quick update. Back at Johannesburg airport and my flight to London seems to be on time so, fingers crossed, landing at Heathrow at about six tomorrow morning.

Had a few hours to kill so have been hitting the airport shops. I would have liked to have bought presents for the BFG in the local market but I didn't have time. I got Freddie a South African football, Georgia a doll in traditional dress and Belle a really nice stuffed elephant. I hope she won't mind, no one seemed to do a cuddly Goliath Tiger Fish!

Leaving Baobab was thankfully uneventful but heart-breaking. It was a beautiful morning when I left, just after dawn is always so tranquil, and the river was already starting to sparkle in the sunshine so that made it even harder to go, especially as I know I will never come back.

I told Grace I didn't want any fuss, but she had still got up early and was waiting in Reception when Thomas picked up my cases and took them to the car. She hugged me so tightly I almost couldn't breathe. She said, 'I am so very sorry to see you go, Anna, you have made the last few months so joyous and have touched all our hearts. We wish you all the happiness you wish yourself.' I think we were both quite close to tears, so I just kissed her, thanked her for her kindness and left as quickly as I could.

I had dreaded seeing Dann but he wasn't there. I had one of those fanciful romantic notions that he would find out I was leaving, race to the airport, whisk me into his arms just before I went into Departures, and say it was all a mistake and that he now realised he was actually in love with me and not Lottie. But, of course, he didn't. I think that stuff only happens in books. The airport was very quiet, like it had just woken up. The only people there were the security staff, a man sweeping the floor, a coffee vendor and about twenty passengers, including me, for the first flight.

I honestly don't know how I feel now. Bruised and hurt and so sad to have left Zambia. I never thought it would touch my heart like it has.

I'll text again when I am home.

Kiss the BFG (and Tom!) for me.

Anna x

Part Three

COMING HOME

October

Email from Izzy to Anna

Hey

Just checking you got home safely? It was great to see you for a few days. I know how tired you have been after all those weeks planning for the wedding. The kids loved having you here. I think Belle starts to look more like you every day.

I didn't want to say anything while you were here, but I think you are starting to look a bit thin. You only picked at your food so I hope you aren't coming down with something?

Anyway, let me know you are back okay when you get this. Even if we eventually end up as two little old ladies living together with a posse of cats in a bungalow in Budleigh Salterton, as your big sis I will always worry about you.

Love

Izzy x

Hey

Back home. The flat felt damp and dreary when I got in but has warmed up nicely now I've turned the heating right up. I used to like the cold but I think those few weeks in Zambia turned me into a bit of a hot-house flower, perhaps now more an African orchid than an English snowdrop?

It was lovely to see you and the children. They are like my reset button. Poor Freddie though, I think he is getting to the squirmy age at the thought of hugging his old auntie. At least Georgia still likes her cuddles though.

And don't worry about me, I'm fine. I like to think I am fashionably slight rather than thin, but whatever you call it, it helps me fit right in to my celebrity circles.

Love

Anna x

Email from Izzy to Anna

Hey

I meant to ask you when you were here, and I know it's a bit early to think about Christmas, but I've just seen an advert with a turkey and a snowman in it, so what the hell. Any plans yet? Robbie is working I think and Mum and Dad are planning to be away, chasing the winter sun as usual. Last time I heard it was a toss-up between Antigua or the Canaries.

You know you are always welcome here. No need to decide just yet but let me know if you want to come to us.

Love

Izzy x

Hey

Thanks sis, that's kind of you to offer. Not sure yet. I may pop down the weekend before to do a present drop if that suits your plans but will probably come back before the festivities begin and just have a quiet few days at home if that is okay.

I don't know what's wrong with me but I'm just not feeling in the mood for all those lights and parties and seasonal bonhomie. Odd really, Matt and I used to enjoy the social scene here at Christmas time but I'm just not sure I'll be in the mood this year.

I'll let you know a bit nearer the time if that is okay?

Oh, any idea what Tom might like for Christmas? Does he still need a new wetsuit, and if so, what size?

Speak soon.

Anna x

Hey

No problem, of course, just let me know when you know.

I'm worried about you, it's not like you to be so blue. It's been nearly four months since you've been home. Is it still Dann?

Izzy x

p.s. Yes please to a wetsuit for Tom, his is really starting to bag at the knees. He likes the ones with the nylon jersey lining. Extra large should be spot on.

I know, stupid and pathetic, right?

What do you think he's doing now? Grace hasn't written for a while and I can't bring myself to write to her in case she gives me some news I don't want to hear. She must think really badly of me, and I don't blame her.

I wonder if Dann and Lottie have talked about marriage? Perhaps it won't be long before they start a family. Remember Grace said their babies would be beautiful and smart, which I am sure would be true. Perhaps they have already left Zambia to go back to Denmark or the Netherlands?

I just wish I could get him out of my head. I keep finding myself holding the rose quartz he gave me, as if that could somehow magically change what has happened.

The good news is that I still write to Henry every week. His letters always lift my spirits. Did I tell you he is going to have a new baby brother or sister soon, which he is very excited about? Oh, and he recently won this year's Spelling Tournament so everyone is super proud of him. He does mention Dann in passing, but luckily most eleven-year-olds have absolutely no interest in their teacher's love life, so I feel like we are on pretty safe ground.

Love

Anna x

Email from Izzy to Anna

Oh, lovely Anna, you are neither stupid nor pathetic, you just fell in love with someone you couldn't have. It will get easier, I promise. If everyone who'd ever been thwarted in love actually died of a broken heart, there'd be no humans left and the world would just be populated by seagulls.

Love

Izzy x

Email from Anna to Izzy

Hey

Thanks, I know you're right, and thanks for making me smile. I do hope it gets easier sooner rather than later – the heartache, that is, not the nightmare of seagull world domination.

I forgot to tell you what I did last month. I'd been out and about visiting some suppliers in the East End, so I decided I'd try to make someone on the tube smile at me by smiling at them first. I know it is a massive no-no in London but I thought, how hard can it be? And September is nearly Christmas, after all!

Well, it turns out harder than I thought. Smartphones and headphones were surely the greatest inventions of our time for keeping one stranger from connecting with another. There was one older gentleman who obviously thought he could survive with just a paper for distraction and he did glance my way, so I smiled my best smile at him. He looked away so quickly I thought I heard his neck snap. I could almost hear him thinking, 'I hope she's not dangerous.'

I told Ellie what I'd done and she looked at me kindly but with an expression that actually said, 'Has she gone mad?'

I know I said I am okay, Izzy, but I'm really not. I don't just miss Dann, I miss Zambia as well. Everyone there smiles at you. Being in London now makes me feel like I did when I first arrived here all those years ago and didn't know anyone and hadn't learned the necessary etiquette to be like every other solitary person here. It is all hustle and bustle, noise and light, and yet I don't think there is anywhere in the world where you can feel more alone.

Just typing this email and see a message has pinged in from Grace after all these months. Perhaps she is a witch after all and knows we have been speaking about her? I may need to go and get a glass of wine to steady my nerves before I open it, just in case.

I'll email you back.

Love Anna x

Email from Grace to Anna

My dearest Anna

It seems like such a long time since I've heard from you. I do miss our correspondence, but I know you have been very busy. I hope you and your husband are enjoying life together once again.

One of our guests left a copy of *Hello!* Magazine in the Observatory when she went home last week, and I saw some of your hats at the royal wedding. They were stunning. That must have been so very exciting for you and your team!

Much has happened here since you left. Has Henry told you that his father and Hester are expecting a baby next spring? It is splendid news, and he has been laughing that her belly will soon become as big as his. Harold is convinced it will be a baby boy. He says, 'Grace, there are too many girls in our family at the moment, and that even includes the hens and the yard dog, so I need to redress the balance for little Henry's sake!' If it is a boy, they have said they will call him Samuel, which is very touching.

Do you remember Brian, our hippo out at Musanga? Well, you can imagine our amazement and shock last month when 'Brian' produced a beautiful little calf, who we have named Namunza, which means 'one born in the afternoon'. As you can imagine, little Namunza is already a firm favourite with my visitors to the island and Brian has duly been renamed Brianna.

Twalumba has finally been fully rebuilt, restocked and reopened, thanks to our lovely supporters and sponsors (and thank you for your donation, it was very generous). We raised more money than we needed, so I asked the ladies what else they would like and they decided on a kiln to make pottery – so we have rebuilt the centre with a new wing and a pottery making area, which is very exciting. They also had enough money left over for a little van, which they have had sign-written 'Twalumba Ladies Co-operative'. Joyce is learning to drive in her husband's bread van so they can take their items to all the local markets without having to ask for help. Patience has applied to take a basic accountancy course so she can help with the bookkeeping, and Joyce and Thelma have met with the Principal at Livingstone Technical College to discuss offering formal qualifications in dress design and tailoring. You would be so proud of how independent they are all becoming.

All the ladies at Twalumba send their warmest and happiest greetings to you. They miss you at the Centre but I hope you will be pleased to learn they are also using all the new skills you taught them to great effect. Betsy's design for our new signature chitenge print with the Baobab Tree motif is proving very popular and we have even had an enquiry about Talu's drawings from a smart gallery up in Lusaka. The ladies have been making all sorts of woven Christmas decorations as well, and the batik tablecloths and place mats with the pied kingfisher design are selling like hot cakes in the Lodge shop.

We have two new university students from Lithuania, Lina and Nojus, who have come to teach biology and maths to our older children until next February, and Lottie has now gone back to Copenhagen. Sadly, my lovely Dann is not in a good place but we are all doing what we can to help him through these difficult months.

Better news to end. I've sold three of Samuel's old cars, but not the Healey. I've kept that – as you know, it was his absolute pride and joy and I could never part with it. Besides, a lady still has to arrive at church in style, don't you think? Mr Alfonso K Sitabele from the local garage gave me a very reasonable price. I was very good friends with his wife Judith before she passed away about ten years ago. It is such a shame that a nice man like Mr Alfonso K Sitabele has been alone for so long.

I've given the money I made from the sale of the cars to Twalumba but have also put a little aside as my contribution to Mwabonwa's special annual fundraiser. This year, they are going to buy new school shoes for every child.

Please do write when you have time. The Lodge, Twalumba and the school haven't been the same since you left. We think about you all the time and miss you. We hope one day you will come back to us.

Your dear friend

Grace x

Email from Anna to Grace

Dear Grace

Thank you for your email, I am so sorry I haven't written for such a long time. Please forgive me. It is no excuse, but you are right – it has been quite hectic here for a couple of months, as you can imagine. Yes, we were very privileged to make a number of the hats for the recent wedding party, including for the bride's mother, which got a lot of attention. I am glad you liked them. Eleanor and I were invited to the ceremony at St Paul's Cathedral, which was an honour and such a special day. We got to wear two of my hats, which hardly ever happens, but of course did not appear personally in any of the style magazines as we are not nearly famous enough. My mother, though, was very proud and I am sure has bored everyone in their village half to death about it. I've attached a photograph here of us before we went into the church so you can see the designs. I hope you like them.

Henry has told me about the new baby, which is wonderful news. He is very excited at the prospect of having a baby brother, but I know he would be as pleased with a baby sister.

What a surprise about Brian/Brianna too! Didn't you

once tell me that umbrella trees were known to boost the fertility of the African soil? If so, it certainly appears to have worked at Musanga.

I'm sorry for Dann's sake that Lottie has gone home but presume not for long? I am not surprised he is miserable as he must be missing her, but I'm sure he will be happy again when she gets back to Mwabonwa, or he goes to Copenhagen, and they are reunited.

Dear friend, I miss Twalumba, I miss the school, I miss the Zambezi and I miss the African night sky, but most of all I miss the people, so I am sending you all my love and best wishes for a happy and peaceful Christmas.

Love
Anna x

Email from Grace to Anna

Dearest Anna

It was so lovely to hear from you.

Yes, we were sorry to say goodbye to Lottie, but she had finished her research and it was time to go home. I don't believe she will be back at Mwabonwa anytime soon, if at all.

I have a confession to make. I know I had held out a fanciful hope that she and Dann may find love together but sadly, I know now that my designs in that direction were completely misplaced. Sometimes I think I am not just foolish and old, but blind as well.

After she left, Dann said that he and Lottie were never anything other than good friends and she already has a partner back in Copenhagen, another academic called Dr Sarah

Larsen. He knew that from her first visit but said she is a very private person and had asked him not to break her confidence. He is right that, for all their goodness and kindness, some people here are not as tolerant as they should be and would not have approved. He told me about their deception. I am a bit cross with him but I know it won't last. I have to say, personally I would have been thrilled to have known about Lottie and Sarah. Despite my meddling, I am, like Emma, first and foremost a believer in love, of whatever shade or hue.

With so much positive news here, it hurts me to see Dann so unhappy. He is working hard and looks tired all the time. These last few months, as soon as he finished teaching, he has been straight out to help the builders with the Centre. I've seen him out there in rain and shine, day and night. Now that the building work is completed, he has said he is going to work on the garden at his cottage, taking out all the native scrub and, with Harold's help, putting in a vegetable garden. That's a huge job but he said he would rather be busy. I sometimes think he doesn't trust himself to have too much time to think.

We all miss you, but I think Dann misses you most of all, although he is far too obstinate to admit it. I secretly think he has found it hard knowing you have reconciled with your husband. He has never admitted it to me, but I often wonder if he had feelings for you all the time? I have told him he should perhaps write to you one last time to make his peace and clear his heart. I hope he does.

And perhaps I wouldn't have given up on you and him so easily if I had known about Lottie as, despite all my interfering nonsense, I still truly believe you and Dann shared some kind of kindred light. However, perhaps a tiny bit of my match-making magic did rub off on you now you are back with your husband, and I am thankful for your happiness, even if it is to the detriment of Dann's.

Do write again soon.

Love

Grace x

Email from Anna to Grace

Dear Grace

Given your honesty, I think I should make a confession too. It's hard for me to write these words as I know I have truly deceived everyone, the people I have come most to care about in the world and whose opinion of me is more important than you will ever know.

When I left Zambia, it wasn't to reunite with my husband. I haven't heard from him in months, certainly from well before I came to work at Twalumba. All I know is that he has moved on from me and I have *definitely* moved on from him.

I came home because I thought Dann loved Lottie, and she him. I couldn't bear to be around them, not because I am mean-spirited or malicious, believe me, but because their happiness was the direct reason for my own unhappiness. Please, please Grace, don't tell him, but I think I have been in love with Dann since before I even came to Zambia, when all I had were words on a page. Could there be some small chance, some tiny grain of hope, that he is in a bad place because of me, because he misses me... because he loves me?

Anna x

p.s. The post has just arrived and there is a letter from Zambia, I recognise Dann's handwriting. I am not sure I want to open it yet. I will write again later.

Letter from Dann to Anna

Dear Anna

It feels so odd writing to you again. I had thought to send an email but it didn't seem right, as I am sure this will be the last time I will write. I think this letter will be long and perhaps painful to read (it certainly will be to write), so I apologise for that but I hope you will indulge me as I now realise it is important that I tell you everything.

Grace says that until I am honest with you, I will never truly find peace, even though I know it is too late for us.

Firstly, I have to apologise for my behaviour towards you over the last week you were here. It was unforgivable. I have no excuses and it is no justification for the way I acted, but perhaps what I am about to write will be something of an explanation. You once asked me to tell you the true story of Dann Huismann, so here it is, in black and white and terrible technicolour.

I want to tell you about what happened with Anika and Aarti, and why I pushed you away so many times even though I spent most of my waking hours thinking of what it would be like to touch you.

I think when we first started to write I made some throwaway comment about being 'broken' in Afghanistan. You never asked and I know I never volunteered any more information. I have spent so many years concealing the truth that it has become second nature to me to put on a front – I think that is how you say it.

I don't remember a lot about that particular day in Uruzgan Province. I know it wasn't long before all our Dutch troops actually pulled out of the country for the last time, and it was a hot and airless afternoon. Our company had received intelligence about a potential cell of insurgents nearby so I took two of my best men, Korporaal Finn Visser and Sergeant Noah Janssen, to walk up to the local village and do a sweep of the houses. These reports were generally baseless, but they all had to be checked out and it was something we had done countless times before.

Finn Visser was very young, only twenty-one. He had very blue eyes and blond hair, and the older soldiers in the unit joked that he looked about twelve years of age so must have enlisted when he was a baby. Despite that, he was a very fine soldier who had shown a lot of promise and had been promoted just before he arrived in Afghanistan for this, his first tour.

We didn't find anyone of interest and so made our way back to camp. For some reason, I was at the back of the line, Finn Visser was at the front and Noah Janssen in the middle. As we started down the hill from the village, Finn stood on a roadside mine and was blown up. I have tried to think of another, more sanitised way to say that, but how can any words describe something so brutal and meaningless?

Finn was killed instantly and Noah Janssen suffered unsurvivable blast trauma and died while he was being transported back to camp. Physically, I was lucky. I suffered some shrapnel injuries to my arms and back and one of my legs was badly broken by flying debris, but I was alive.

I wasn't in any pain but I was floating in and out of consciousness and I could hear a lot of shouting. I vividly remember the acrid smell of smoke burning my throat and seeing Finn Visser's outstretched arm on the ground beside me, still holding his sunglasses in his hand but with no body above the shoulder. It is so odd the images that stick in your mind.

Within twenty-four hours, I was evacuated back to the Netherlands. The doctors at the military hospital were able to save my leg and patch me up so that you would almost never know I had been injured.

The only problem was that, while my body was healing, my mind wasn't. It was my fault Finn and Noah died. I was their commanding officer and should have been leading. Not only was there crushing guilt, but I had seen things that I couldn't get out of my head, and they seemed to play over and over and over like they were on some terrible loop and there was no stop button. There was counselling offered, which I took, but I deteriorated quite badly and was sent to a military mental facility for three months.

When I started to feel a bit better I was allowed home and was eventually medically discharged from the army. By that time, Anika and I had been married for six years, and it wasn't long after my return that Aarti was born. Anika and I had been childhood sweethearts and she had all the qualities that made her an amazing army wife. She was kind and patient and was able to bear the long periods of separation that many soldiers and their families have to endure. Aarti was a real daddy's boy. He was fair like Anika but he had my eyes.

Once home, I threw myself into studying, having decided that I would become a teacher. But the nightmares never went away, however much I tried to push them down or pretend they weren't there.

On the surface life seemed to be good, but underneath I was falling apart.

Anika and I started to argue, just bickering at first and then full-scale shouting matches. I know we were both worried about Aarti growing up in such a toxic atmosphere but I couldn't stop myself. Anika was totally blameless, of course, but I was just so angry all the time.

On the night they died, I was driving the car. Most people here at Mwabonwa know my family were killed in a car accident, but only Grace and Samuel knew I was the driver. It was a very wet Sunday in November. Aarti – who was about four by then – was a bit restless and bored and Anika and I had been arguing all day. I can't even remember what about now, all the fights seem to have merged into one.

Anika had packed an overnight bag and said she was going to take Aarti to her mother's for a few days to give me time to cool down. I didn't want her driving such a long way in the rain so said I would take them and pick them up later that week.

The rest is a bit of a blur. We were still arguing when we were hit by a lorry that swerved across our lane. Anika and Aarti were killed instantly, but I survived with just a few cuts and bruises. At the inquest, it transpired that the lorry driver had suffered a heart attack at the wheel and the coroner said that no blame was apportioned to me, but of course I did blame myself and have done so every day since that time. The twists of fate are cruel. If I had been in front of my men in Afghanistan, as I should have been, and been killed, Anika and Aarti would still be alive today.

And on the day they died, what if I had been driving more slowly? Would those few seconds have been enough for me to see the danger and swerve out of the way? What if I had been going faster and all I saw was a lorry heading for the opposite ditch in my rear-view mirror? And, fundamentally, would Anika have even wanted to go that night if I had been a better husband?

It was then I really hit rock bottom. I truly believed I had the blood of four people on my hands. Two that I liked and greatly respected, and two that I loved – and still love – with every fibre of my being. For most of the year after Anika and Aarti died, I was the lowest any man can be without taking the ultimate step and ending it all. And believe me, there were many times I contemplated it. The only comfort I had was that Aarti was asleep in the back seat when the accident happened. If he had been crying or frightened because we were arguing, and he sometimes had been in his short life, I know I would have had no hesitation in ending my own life. If that was the last image I ever had of him, I know I wouldn't have been able to bear it.

I was in a very deep, black hole that I could see no way out of. I started to drink heavily and did many other things that I am not proud of. My mother and father were amazing and patient, even though they were grieving the loss of their daughter-in-law and their much-loved only grandchild. They took me home to live with them in Alkmaar and, very slowly, I thought I could see a tiny chink of light in the darkness.

It's then that I saw the advert looking for a Geography Teacher at Mwabonwa. I was newly qualified and had no experience, and it was plain for anyone to see that I was quite unwell, so I honestly didn't think I would even be considered, but it seemed like it could be a fresh start away from home and the misery and pain I had caused.

I called the number on the advertisement and by chance, and to my eternal good fortune, Samuel answered. In the end, we spoke for over an hour. I don't know why but I just poured out everything that had happened – it was like a dam had broken and I couldn't stop. Samuel was quiet and just listened, and then I clearly remember him saying, 'Mr Huismann, I can hear you are deeply troubled and have suffered a terrible loss, but God will not judge you as you judge yourself, and neither will we. Why don't you come for a month to see if you like it here? No obligation.' So that is what I did.

And I do truly believe Zambia has healed me. It was a long road but every day that has passed, the stillness and beauty of this place helped mend so much in me that was broken. I still kept my deepest secrets and sometimes had nightmares in the early years, but the guilt and pain began to have less and less hold over me and I started to find real peace.

And then Miss Anna Peel came into my life.

From the first time we wrote, I thought you were funny and kind. I also saw the photo you sent to Henry and thought you were incredibly beautiful.

Your letters made me smile and I found myself increasingly looking forward to receiving each new correspondence and to writing back. Feeling a little jolt in my chest every time the email pinged was a new, exciting and – frankly – scary sensation for me. It felt liberating to laugh and flirt with a woman again, even if it was only in print.

Then, one night last February, I remember lying in bed listening to the rain and I couldn't get you out of my head…

and I realised that, for the first time in six years, I hadn't thought about Anika or Aarti all day.

It was then I got scared. It felt like they were slipping away from me and, however much I hated the pain, the guilt was like an evil twin that was suffocating me but sustaining me at the same time. Perhaps that is how addicts feel when they give up their drugs. They want to be clean but they are frightened of life without the one thing they can rely on, however much it is killing them.

That is why I wrote to tell you I didn't think we should correspond anymore. I was so stupid, but I thought that I would be better being on my own rather than loving someone again who I could hurt, or who could hurt me.

And then Grace said you were coming to teach at Twalumba.

That took a lot of resolve on my part. Luckily, or unluckily, I have got so used to hiding my feelings in the shadows that it was fairly easy to fool myself into believing I was indifferent to you when you arrived. But sometimes I just couldn't stop myself wanting to be with you.

Do you remember that Sunday on the river? I know Grace wanted me to take Lottie, but I was so happy when she turned me down as I was desperate to spend some time with you, even though I knew I was playing with emotional fire. It was truly one of the happiest days of my life, just you and me out on the water. I think of it all the time.

And, despite my outward disinterest, there were so many times I just wanted to touch you and blurt out my real feelings. Do you think when I found you in my bedroom that day I wanted to reject you? I felt as if there was some invisible bond between us and didn't think I was imagining the electricity I felt, so it took all of my will and resolve not to reach for you. I remember the sick feeling in the pit of my stomach when you left, even though I still thought I was doing the right thing. Every day, I thought I would reset and just look on you like a friend, like Lottie, and then every day I saw you I was right back to square one.

And then we kissed and I spent four days making myself believe it was meaningless, still denying to myself that I was in love with you. You were right to be angry with me when I came to see you. It is unconscionable that by saying having a casual relationship wasn't my style, I was somehow implying it was yours. In my defence, I wonder now whether what I meant got lost in translation, but I knew I could never have a meaningless relationship with you, even though every fibre of my being would have taken that if it had been the only way I could have been close to you.

And when I was ill, I remember you sitting with me all night in the hospital. I think I was a bit out of it (is that the right term?) but I remember just listening to your voice and feeling your hand in mine. I knew that, despite every angry word we had exchanged and every barrier I had put up, then was the time for honesty. So I remember saying 'I love you,' but I don't remember much after that and the next day you were gone. When I got back to the Lodge you seemed to be avoiding me, so I started to worry that I had completely misjudged the situation, which I knew I had when you told Grace you were going back to England early to be reunited with your husband.

So, I hope you will forgive me. If my behaviour towards you was cool and sometimes confusing, or my actions embarrassed you in any way, I wanted you to know why. I had spent many months feeling like a spinning magnet – sometimes an invisible force was pulling me to you, other times repelling me from you, and there was nothing I could do to stop it.

Anna, please believe me when I say I never wanted to hurt you. I was just desperately trying to find a way to protect myself from falling in love with you and, as you now know, that was utterly futile.

I think maybe if I had been more honest with you at the beginning, it could have turned out differently, and for that I blame only myself. If it is any consolation, the pain I feel now is totally due to my own stupidity and pig-headedness.

I think that is all I can say. I am sorry this letter is so long. It is late and my hand is starting to cramp so I will end now.

Although it has ended this way, you gave me hope and I will always be grateful for your friendship.

I wish you and your husband all the very best for a happy and peaceful future together.

Dann x

Email from Anna to Grace

Dear Grace

I've just read Dann's letter.

He has told me everything about Anika and Aarti and what happened to him in Afghanistan. Why didn't you tell me?

Anna x

Email from Grace to Anna

My dearest Anna

You know why I couldn't. It wasn't for me or anyone else to tell you. You would only ever hear the true and complete story of Dann Huismann from Dann Huismann himself.

I now realise it is stupid of me to think I can ever bring two people together. Only they truly have the power to do so.

I hope you will forgive me.

Grace x

Email from Anna to Grace

Dear Grace

There is nothing to forgive and perhaps it is me who should be asking for forgiveness. I don't think either of us wanted to deceive you, I think we were just deceiving ourselves. Dann says he loves me, Grace. I am so confused. What should I do?

Email from Grace to Anna

My dearest, loveliest Anna

Do you really need to ask? Come home and tell him.

Grace x

❉

Email from Anna to Grace

Dear Grace

I've just booked my flights. I don't have time to wait for a visa so will get it at the airport when I arrive. Barring any major delays, I should be arriving into Livingstone the day after tomorrow at about 3 o'clock, off the Johannesburg flight. Would you be able to send Thomas to pick me up? If not, don't worry, I am sure I can find a taxi when I get there.

Also, I am not sure how long I will be staying – I think that depends on what happens with Dann – but do you have any rooms available at the Lodge? I know it is very short notice and you are probably very busy, but I am happy of course to pay whatever's appropriate. If not, can you recommend any of the neighbouring properties or, failing that, a hotel in town?

Love

Anna x

Email from Grace to Anna

Dear Anna

Of course I will send Thomas to collect you, and don't be silly, I wouldn't have you stay anywhere else but Baobab. We are full at the moment but I insist you stay with me. I will ask Sarah to make up the guest suite ready.

What about Dann? Do you want me to tell him you are coming?

Love

Grace x

Email from Anna to Grace

Dear Grace

Thank you for everything, you are a very dear friend.

I've thought long and hard about whether to contact Dann before I come. It would be so easy just to drop him an email, but somehow that just doesn't seem right for something so important. What would I say? 'Hello Dann, thanks for your letter, I love you too'?! Something inside me says I have to see him face to face to know if what was truly in his heart when he wrote to me is still there. It's a long way to come, I know, and every hour until I get there will be agony. Perhaps I will be rejected and I will have to bear that as best as I can, but I think it's the right thing to do.

Anna x

Email from Grace to Anna

Anna

Of course I won't tell him if that is your wish but please believe what I am about to tell you.

I have known Dann for nearly six years now. He has many faults and he is by no means perfect. He can be stubborn and you know now, better than anyone, the demons he battles.

But one thing I do know for certain is that he knows his own mind. Falling in love with you wouldn't have been easy for him, and I am not surprised he kept it so well hidden, not just from you but from himself. I am sure he is scared but if he said he loves you, he loves you, and four months apart won't have done anything to change that.

I so look forward to having you home with us all in Zambia. I will pray for your safe arrival.

Love Grace x

✽

Email from Anna to Izzy

Hi sis

I've had a letter from Dann. Too much to explain and to be honest, I am still processing it myself.

I just wanted to let you know I am going to Zambia tomorrow. There is something I have to tell him.

Love Anna x

p.s. Don't worry.

Email from Izzy to Anna

Anna

Tomorrow!! I hope it's what I think it can only be! Let me know when you get there and what happens. I have everything crossed for you.

Love Izzy x

Email from Anna to Ellie

Hi Ellie

Please don't think I've gone mad, but I am going to Zambia tomorrow. Important business. Can you clear my diary until the weekend at the earliest please? I'll email or phone you again later in the week to explain.

Love

Anna

✽

Email from Anna to Izzy

Hey sis

Arrived safe and sound. Just settling in at Grace's before dinner, so will catch you up briefly, but no cheating and reading the end of this email first to find out what has happened!

Thomas picked me up at the airport and as we pulled into the Lodge, I could see Grace pacing up and down in the Reception area. I jumped out of the car but we didn't exchange pleasantries, no 'How was your flight?' or 'It's good to be back.' I just hugged her briefly and said, 'Where is he?'

She said that school had finished for the day and she was fairly sure he was back at his cottage, no doubt working in his garden, as he seemed to do each evening until it was too dark to see.

It felt so odd, yet so right, to be back here again, even though I hardly looked at the people or the river. I walked as quickly as I could through the grounds, skirted round the edge of the new Twalumba buildings and then down the long winding path to Dann's cottage.

When I got to the gate, I could see him at the far side of his garden with his back to me, digging. After not seeing him for so long, I genuinely thought my heart was going to stop. Honestly, Izzy, it felt as if someone was moving a grand piano from the pit of my stomach to my chest and back again.

As I pushed open the gate, the hinges rasped and Dann looked up. I am not sure how long we stared at each other – it could have been five hours or five minutes or five seconds. I took a step forward but Dann dropped his spade and crossed the distance between us in four strides. He stopped just inches from me and I could see every pore on his beautiful, kind face that I love so very much.

He looked totally confused and shocked, as if he had seen a ghost or one of Piet's Zambezi river spirits, so I just said, 'Dann Huismann, you went to a lot of effort to write to me to tell me you loved me, so I thought it was only fair that I should make the effort to travel 7,296 miles to tell you I love you too.'

The next bit is something of a blur. What I said seemed to sink in and suddenly he had the biggest smile on his face I have ever seen (OMG, his smile makes me go weak at the knees!). There was a lot of kissing, holding and touching, and a few tears from both of us.

We stood like that for about five minutes. There is so much to explain, but there will be time for that. It wasn't long before we heard the sound of singing coming down the path and Grace, Harold and Hester came into view. Hester was holding Henry's hand, obviously to stop him running ahead, but when he saw me he broke free, ran through the gate and clung to me so tightly I nearly fell over. Harold and Hester looked very pleased to see me, although they are less demonstrable, as is the custom here. Harold had a basket of fruit from his garden and Hester was holding a small package wrapped in a scrap of fabric tied with a raffia bow.

When Grace saw Dann and I in each other's arms, she obviously knew it was good news. She rushed forward too and embraced Dann, then me, then Dann again, then both of us at the same time. Poor little Henry didn't seem to mind being squashed between us. I think we were all crying by then, but they were happy tears.

Hester gestured for Henry to come back. She whispered something to him and gave him the package, which he gave to me. He looked very solemn but when I opened it, Harold broke into a huge smile and started to clap his hands and dance. It was the painted 'Do Not Disturb' sign from their bedroom door. Harold rubbed Hester's pregnant belly (she has the most perfect baby bump) and said, 'We won't be needing this for a while so we thought you would have more use for it.' Henry said to Grace, in case she needed an explanation, 'Daddy says if I see the sign hanging on the gate, I mustn't go in because Mr Huismann and Miss Anna might be kissing.'

And then Henry said in a very serious tone, 'Mr Huismann, are you going to marry Miss Anna?' He just smiled and said, 'We'll see.'

Love

Anna x

Email from Izzy to Anna

Anna

Tom and I are absolutely delighted for you both.

Thank God you didn't travel 7,296 miles (I won't ask how you know that!) and he had already got over you. Joking, of course. Notwithstanding the aberration that is Matt the Ratt, once someone loves you, honestly Anna, how could they ever *not* love you?

Oh, and BTW, are you?

Izzy x

Email from Anna to Izzy

Am I what?

Email from Izzy to Anna

Going to become Mrs Huismann?

Email from Anna to Izzy

In the words of the man I love and who loves me (I can't even believe I'm typing those words!) - 'We'll see.'

❊

Hey

Still on Cloud 9 this morning. It feels odd and strange but utterly wonderful all at the same time. I've just finished breakfast. Grace agrees with you that I am too thin, but I seem to have got my appetite back a bit this morning and will probably be the size of a house soon! Isn't that what contentment does to you? Thought you would like a quick update before I go over to see Dann.

Grace is still insistent I stay with her for the time being and, of course, I am going to respect her wishes, although I'm not sure how I survived six months without Dann. Now six minutes seems like five and a half minutes too long! Anyway, it was odd lying in Grace's guest bed last night, knowing he was so close. There was such a lot running through my head, and his too I think, that I imagine neither of us got much sleep.

Last night was really magical though. Yesterday Grace said, 'You two have a lot to talk about, so let me arrange a private dinner at the Lodge.' Well, she really went to town. The Observatory is often used in the evening for guests to have a special dining experience as they look out high over the Zambezi, but she had moved all the other diners into the main restaurant so that we would have it to ourselves. It's decorated with a thousand fairy lights so looks really pretty.

Dann came to 'pick me up' at 8 o'clock, just like a proper date. He had trimmed his beard and looked freshly scrubbed, even if his trousers looked like they could do with a bit of a press. He smelt lovely. I had on that floaty yellow cotton teadress, do you remember the one, it has little daisies and cornflowers on it? Very simple but sort of felt right for the occasion. I think we both felt like nervous teenagers but that is okay.

The meal was lovely but I apologised to Grace as we hardly ate any of it. She said she totally understood. She knows that new love fills you up so there is very little room for anything else.

We talked and talked and talked until about midnight, and then Dann 'walked me home'. Nothing else happened (there will be plenty of time for that) but let's just say it was quite hard saying goodnight – he is a great kisser for a geography teacher!

Love Anna xxx

p.s. Oh, and you were right. Last year's 'incident' with the storm, the post and the bedroom encounter had much more to do with unfulfilled desire than the weather!

Email from Izzy to Anna

Hi back

Ha!! Knew I was right, you need to learn to trust your big sister's instincts.

What happened with Lottie?

Izzy x

Email from Anna to Izzy

Hey

Lottie's now back in Copenhagen and I don't think has any plans to return to Zambia. Of course, I asked him about her before anything else.

He said that when she came to Mwabonwa the first time, they hit it off straight away. He was interested in her research work and mostly understood it, which was a bonus. He found out that her grandparents are actually Dutch and live in Huisberg, which isn't far from Maastricht. She knew the area well growing up. He said that although he isn't nearly as clever as her, he did have the benefit of local knowledge and experience, so he was a really useful sounding board for her work.

He said that it wasn't long after they met, probably two or three weeks, that she told him she had a serious girlfriend back in Denmark. She wanted to be true to herself but wasn't keen on sharing that information more widely. He said we are used to our European liberalism, and nearly everyone he's met in Zambia is tolerant, but some are less so, and Lottie didn't want any distractions from her research.

Then he said that when Grace asked her about any 'significant other', Lottie was quite vague and, not long after, Grace started to introduce her to all the single men she knew... even lovely Mr Alfonso K Sitabele who comes to the Lodge to service all the vehicles, and he must be at least seventy!

Dann said he told Lottie about Grace's genuinely kind but insatiable appetite to see people happy, in love and preferably married, so they hatched a simple plan. He would pretend to like Lottie romantically, and she him, which they thought would keep them both from any more awkward introductions, at least while Lottie was at Mwabonwa.

Anna x

Email from Izzy to Anna

But didn't you say Grace had seen them kissing? Was that true?

Izzy

Email from Anna to Izzy

Yes she had, but it was just another piece of choreographed theatre solely for Grace's benefit, I'm afraid. Dann feels really guilty now for deceiving her, but he thinks she has a forgiving nature and will be too wrapped up in the excitement that he has eventually found love with me to worry about how their ruse temporarily threw her off course.

Dann said he and Lottie bumped into each other over by the Observatory one morning and she was asking him for his opinion on something when he saw Grace in the nearby shrubbery. She had some secateurs in her hand and looked like she was doing some pruning. Even though she appeared not to have noticed them, it seemed such a curious thing to see her there that Dann just knew she was actually more interested in spying on them than deadheading her bougainvillea.

On impulse, Dann whispered to Lottie. 'Grace is watching, shall we kiss?' – which they did, briefly. Obviously satisfied by what she had seen, Grace moved on, at which point Lottie apparently wiped her mouth with the back of her hand and said, 'Let's never do that again, it was horrible.' Dann says they have both laughed about it since.

Love Anna x

Email from Izzy to Anna

But what about him saying, 'I love you, Lottie' in the hospital?

Email from Anna to Izzy

He was genuinely a bit baffled by that. He said he absolutely knew it was me when he said 'I love you', although the doctor told him later that he had been feverish and delirious, so it's not really surprising he can't remember why he then said Lottie's name. He thinks perhaps he was going to say something like 'Lottie and I are just friends' or 'Lottie isn't the one who keeps me awake at night thinking about her'. Anyway, it doesn't matter now.

He said he knew it was me because he quite clearly remembers listening to me recounting all sorts of family stories just for something to say. He said if he hadn't been so out of it, he would have laughed out loud when I told him the silly story of you and me stuck in that hotel lift in Sardinia with a feral cat and nothing to defend ourselves but two sunhats!

Anna x

*

Email from Anna to Izzy

Hi sis

Dann is teaching this morning, so I went over to the Arts Centre to surprise my ladies. I stood in the doorway for about thirty seconds just watching them working – it was bustling with women and the air was full of chatter and laughter. Then Thelma looked up and spotted me, and literally squealed. They all rushed over, hugging me and speaking all at the same time, saying, 'When did you get here, Miss Anna?', 'How long are you staying?' and 'Why are you back home with us?' I just said, 'I'm going to marry Mr Huismann, the geography teacher at Mwabonwa, but don't tell him I've told you as he hasn't asked me yet.' There were a lot of smiling, happy faces at my news!

After all the hugging and hubbub had died down, Joyce and Thelma gave me a tour of the new centre. It is certainly very impressive, about twice the size of the original building and at least six times bigger than Grace's garage! They have a large separate annex now which they use as the crèche they always wanted, with each of the ladies on a rota to look after the babies.

They also have a separate area for their new pottery venture, as Grace said in her letter, complete with two potter's wheels and an outside kiln. Joyce says they have a local potter come in once a week (his name is Edwin Potter – seriously!) who has been teaching them the art of coil pot making, throwing pots, slips, glazes and firing. It turns out Patience is a most skilled pupil and has already made some really pretty tableware.

With all this additional space, Grace and a delegation from the Centre went to see Dr Nkosi, who is the Medical Director at Livingstone Hospital and also happens to be the brother of the school librarian. They persuaded him to second one of their female doctors to come to the Centre every second week to hold a women's health clinic. Henry's cousin Milimo is going to help the new doctor with her admin and record-keeping while she waits for confirmation of her place at university to study medicine. She says it will look good on her CV.

It was lovely to see Talu again, and Mazala was there too, fixing one of the broken sewing machines. He has a brand-new wheelchair that Talu paid for from the sale of her drawings and they say they hope that in about six months they will have saved enough money to travel to Lusaka to buy him a specially made prosthetic leg. Their little son Precious is now crawling around and they let me hold their baby daughter. She is nearly four months old and totally gorgeous. They have named her Anna. Talu said, 'I never wanted to forget how you helped me find my voice,' which nearly made me cry.

Love

Anna x

✳

Hi Ellie

Are you free if I call you? I've got some news to tell you and I need to ask you something important.

    Love

    Anna x

Email from Anna to Izzy

Hey sis

Hope everything okay at home.

All good here. Did I say good? I meant wonderful and amazing!

It's a school day so Dann has been teaching since 9 o'clock, so I said I would run some errands in town for Grace. I'm getting quite expert at driving the Lodge van and even those fierce-looking guards at the check-point now wave 'hello' when I go by.

When I got back, I thought I would wander over and see Dann teaching. Nothing makes me happier. He asks if it is because I am so impressed by his academic knowledge, and I say, 'No, it's because of your glasses,' lol.

Anyway, today he was in one of the open-sided classrooms so I stopped to watch him for a while. He suddenly said, 'Excuse me for a moment, class,' and came over to where I was standing. I thought he was going to ask me a question, but he just pulled me to him and kissed me so passionately that I think we both forgot where we were for a moment until all the children starting climbing on their chairs to see what their teacher was doing, whooping, hollering, clapping and screaming with laughter. Then, calmly as you like, he said, 'Right, you lot, back to glacial moraines and alluvial deposit systems.'

Love

Anna x

Email from Izzy to Anna

Anna

I can't tell you how pleased I am for you both. There are so many questions though, I don't know where to start. Are you going to stay in Zambia?

Izzy

Email from Anna to Izzy

Hey

Well, my tourist visa will take me to the early new year. Grace is going to speak to the Town Hall in Livingstone to see if she can fast-track a work permit for me so I can stay longer. She is fairly confident she can. She says Twalumba has grown so much since it opened and the funds are looking healthy, so it's probably a good time to employ some proper staff. Joyce is looking forward to being the new Principal, but they are also thinking of advertising for the post of Head of Creative Teaching, which I would like to apply for.

Honestly, though, I don't care what I do as long as I can help them. If they insist on giving me a wage, I will probably gift it back to the Centre anyway. It will help to pay Joyce's salary.

Love

Anna x

Email from Izzy to Anna

What will you do with your flat?

Email from Anna to Izzy

All arranged. I've already spoken to Ellie. I remember last month she mentioned that her younger sister Chloe was desperate to find a place in town. She's still living at home but has just got her first job at an architect's firm in Vauxhall and it's a long commute each day from Teddington. Ellie has already asked her if she would like to rent my flat and she's jumped at the chance. It's a short hop across the river so in a perfect location, I'm asking a fair rent for fully furnished and I've only made one stipulation – that she waters my pot plants! Ellie is pleased too. She says Chloe is a very responsible young woman, but it will mean she is much closer to her so she can keep a watchful eye on her too, young woman being let loose in the big city for the first time and all that.

Love

Anna x

Email from Izzy to Anna

And your business?

Email from Anna to Izzy

I also spoke to Ellie about that, and I've offered her a partnership. I think Peel Alberon Millinery has a nice ring about it, don't you? I know she's ready for it and she was delighted. I can still do my design work from here – in fact, I'm getting such a lot of inspiration from the women at Twalumba, but also the wildlife and landscape, I think my flagging creative juices are going to be supercharged for next season. This way, I can continue to do what I love and she can step up to run the business day-to-day and do all the client interfacing. Honestly, she is a million times better at it than me anyway, so I know she will do an amazing job.

Love

Anna x

Email from Izzy to Anna

Are you sure you want to throw it all away to be a geography teacher's wife in Africa?

Email from Anna to Izzy

Not throw it away, give it away gladly.

p.s. And, technically, he hasn't asked me yet.

Email from Izzy to Anna

Sorry, that did sound harsh, but you know what I mean. Playing devil's advocate a bit, but I just want to be sure you are sure. You must be proud of what you've achieved?

Izzy x

Email from Anna to Izzy

Hey

Of course I'm proud. I had my own successful business before I was thirty and when I see one of my hats on the head of a famous woman, it does give me a lovely sense of achievement. But it isn't, and never was, the lifestyle I wanted for myself. I suppose success brought some sort of low-level fame and meant I mixed in certain circles, but it was never a place I felt comfortable, you know that.

Going to Fashion Week in Paris or New York or spending endless hours at celebrity fittings must sound very glamorous to many people, but actually it was just a hard slog. I've met some lovely, genuine people but also a lot of shallow, entitled people. Perhaps Matt was right after all. I don't think I had 'imposter syndrome' because I didn't think my talents were worthy enough, but because I didn't fit into that world and, frankly, never wanted to. Do you know, last year a certain celebrity (I can't name them) asked me to make three identical hats in three slightly different shades of pink as she wasn't sure which she liked best? That was thousands of pounds wasted, easily enough to fund a new teacher at Mwabonwa, buy a new minibus or pay for all the children's cultural visits for several years!

When I think of achievements in my life, it is my small contribution to the Ladies of Twalumba that makes me the proudest. They have very little but by working together, they have been able to realise their amazing talent. Did you know, a gallery in Lusaka is interested in buying Talu's drawings and she is happy, not because of any fame or fortune, but because she can now pay to send her two children to school, buy them shoes and put food on the table every night without worrying. Oh, and get Mazala a prosthetic leg, of course!

I know all that might sound a bit worthy and earnest, but it is true. Every little thing I have achieved here makes me happier than any of the big things I achieved in London.

Love

Anna x

Email from Izzy to Anna

Well, if you are absolutely 100% sure, I am sure too. 😊

Izzy x

Email from Anna to Izzy

Lovely sis

Thank you for caring, I have never been more sure about anything in my entire life. I love Dann with every fibre of my being, so where he is, I have to be.

He did say he would leave Zambia and come back to London with me if that is what I wanted, but I can't think of anything I would like to do less. My heart is here, not just because of Dann but because of Africa.

It's so hard to explain in words, but I feel a constant deep vibration in my chest, a weird resonance connecting me to everything here. I told Dann and he says he has the same feeling, like the rumbling of a thousand water buffalo hooves in the distance. Don't laugh, but perhaps something primordial has called me back to an African home I never knew I had. I know that looks fanciful when I write it down, but I don't know how else to express it or explain it.

Love

Anna x

✻

Email from Anna to Izzy

Hey sis

Thought I would drop you a quick email. Dann is in the shower and I am lying in his bed (don't get overexcited, I know you!), listening to the rain pounding on the tin roof.

When I came down to the cottage earlier, I opened the door and Dann was standing by the mantelpiece above his fireplace, just setting down the photo of Anika and Aarti I had picked up from his bedside table all those months ago. I looked at him, and he looked at me, and I think we both knew now was the right time. He said, 'Shall I put the sign on the gate?' I just nodded as I didn't trust myself to say anything else.

I always think of him as so sure and fearless, but when he came back inside, he looked at me with such a serious expression that I was scared for a moment. He said, 'It's been five years since I've been with a woman. I hope I haven't forgotten what to do.'

Izzy, I know you tell me everything, and I tell you everything, and you will want more details, but just this once you aren't getting them – but let's just say, he hadn't!

Love

Anna x

Email from Izzy to Anna

Anna

Bear with, I'm using my imagination. Getting hints of unadulterated passion and long pent-up desire, am I close? Are those gorgeous arms as strong as I first thought? Is he secretly ripped under all that khaki? I've never pashed a man with a beard, does it tickle?

Love

Izzy xx

Email from Anna to Izzy

Yes, Yes, Yes and Yes!

Anna xx

✹

Hey

Just packing my bag as I'm going to move into Dann's cottage. It isn't going to take me more than five minutes as I wasn't sure how long I would be staying so I came with hardly any luggage, just a carry-on. Once I'm settled, I'm going to treat myself to a trip into Livingstone with Esther to buy a new wardrobe (the fabric kind, not the wood kind!). Nothing fancy, just enough to get me through the next few weeks.

I was a bit apprehensive about telling Grace. I don't know why but I thought she wouldn't approve. I don't want to abuse her hospitality by outstaying my welcome in her guest suite, however lovely it is, and I'm spending so much time with Dann now, it makes sense. And, of course, I just want to go to sleep with him every night and wake up next to him every morning.

I was pleasantly surprised by her reaction when I told her though – she just said, 'Of course you must, he's been alone for too long. She took both of my hands in hers and said, 'One thing I've learned from Samuel's death is that life is short and every moment you can be with the one person you truly love is a precious blessing and should never be taken for granted. But don't leave it too long and tell him that if he hasn't asked you within a month, I will be very cross with him.'

She made me smile when she added, 'Anyway, having a woman's touch in that cottage will be a good thing. Perhaps you can persuade him to change those dreary curtains.'

Oh, more good news. Grace is going out to dinner next week with Mr Alfonso K Sitabele who owns the local garage (the man she tried to introduce to Lottie, remember?!). I met him once. He is quite reserved but utterly charming. Grace says it is just dinner, but you never know…

Love

Anna x

Email from Izzy to Anna

Just a serious thought, presume you've found the right moment to talk to Dann about his wife and son?

Email from Anna to Izzy

Hi

Yes, I don't want it ever to be something unspoken between us. I've told him that he can talk to me about Anika and Aarti whenever he wants to and to share every memory he has of them. Even if I could, I would never want to replace them and I will never be jealous of the love he still has for both of them. Why would I be?

In an ideal world, we would never have met. Dann would have got better, he and Anika would have worked out their problems, had more children and lived an uneventful life in the Netherlands. I would have been the love of Matt's life and he would never have left me. But none of that happened and we are where we are, not through any design but by twists and turns that neither of us could ever have predicted.

But Zambians believe in fate and there have been so many forks in the road that have led me and Dann to be here today, in this place and at this point in time, so we are just going to embrace this magical, unseen force that has brought us together, however painful the journey.

Oh, and do you remember, you once asked me if Dann was actually, literally perfect? The answer is no, he's just a man, and a flawed one at that. But he is actually, literally perfect enough for me.

Love

Anna x

✤

Email from Anna to Izzy

Izzy

I know it might seem like a crazy idea but why don't you give your annual pilgrimage to your in-laws a miss next year and come over to Zambia in the summer holidays? It's a lovely time to visit, dry and a bit cooler. Perhaps Freddie and Georgia might be a bit young for all the travelling, but I know Tom's parents would be thrilled to still have them visit for a couple of weeks and Belle would love it here. I've already suggested it to Grace and she would be delighted to offer you a place to stay. Grace says Dann is her family, I am now Dann's family and you are my family, so that makes us all family in the eyes of Zambians.

Come and meet Dann and the wonderful people here and see this magical place for yourself, and then you will know why I am so in love with him, them and it.

Say yes!

Love Anna

p.s. I will even ask Piet to take Belle out on the river to try to catch a tiger fish (a small one!).

January

Letter from Belle Rowbottom to Henry Sissonga

Hello Henry

Belle's word of the day for Henry: LOGOPHILE

My name is Belle, which is short for Belinda. Anna Peel is my aunt. Auntie Anna says she thinks you are missing having a friend to write to now you see her nearly every day, so she has asked if I would write to you.

I am nearly twelve years of age and I am just starting my second term at senior school. I like drawing, wildlife and reading. When I am older, I would like to be a wildlife artist, marine biologist or an environmental scientist, although I haven't decided which yet. Auntie Anna let me read your letter on Zambian snakes – it was very interesting. She says you used to want to be an explorer but are now thinking about being an English teacher or a journalist. She says you like words, so I have chosen a suitable word for the day above. I hope you like it. It means someone who likes words.

My mum and dad are trying to arrange a visit to Zambia

in the school holidays this summer, which I am very excited about as I have heard all about it from Auntie Anna. My mum is very happy that she is going to marry your teacher Mr Huismann. Auntie Anna told my mum that Mr Huismann proposed to her in front of the whole school in assembly one morning, is that true? Yuk, how embarrassing! My mum says she will 'bring hats' although my dad wasn't sure they would have enough room in our luggage. I have a younger brother and sister, but they are too little to come so will be spending the holidays with my grandad and grandma.

Auntie Anna taught me to play chess last year and she says she is teaching you too, so I hope we can play when I visit. Do you get confused about which way the knight can move? I know I do, but it is still my favourite piece on the board.

If you would like to be my pen-pal, I would like that very much.

I hope you write soon.

Your new friend.

Belle Rowbottom

Aged 11 ¾